The Hitman's Dilemma

By: Ricky Hood

Table of Contents

It was not a surprise when both of the shots hit their targets with unparalleled accuracy. What was shocking was that the person behind the trigger was nothing more than a fourteen year old boy who was well-trained and refused to miss. Logan Aster had been handling guns of a variety of looks and sizes since he was all of seven years of age, and as the years passed more quickly than he would have liked, he became better and more accurate with using them. By the time he was ten, he was able to hit a target infallibly from distances as far as several hundred meters.

Able Lock would have been proud of how well he had taken the advice, and how much of the vital information he had absorbed before being given his first mission, for lack of a better term. Able had come into his life one cold, winter night when his best friend had met his end in the worst way imaginable. Logan had been hiding under the bed in his mother and father's room when the three armed men, young men in reality around 20 years of age, entered and tied up Martin and Judith Aster. They spent the whole night tormenting and torturing them before shooting them both execution style in the back of the head and leaving without another word. Logan had heard every second of the confrontations from his hiding place and the fact that he could do nothing to prevent it from happening made him feel emotions that he didn't even know existed until that moment.

When the call had gone over the scanners after Logan called emergency services, a listening Able Lock happened to hear it and recognized the address that belonged to his closest friend. He was quick to jump up from his recliner in his sparsely decorated living room in the dilapidated house in the woods to race to the location and do what he could. He found Logan, the only child in the family, out back in a tree house that no one knew existed, huddled under a blanket and shivering both from the cold and the sensations. He gently and cautiously climbed up the stairs leading into the single room in the tiny structure and slowly approached the boy. Logan recognized him and crawled over to him on his hands and knees and then slid into his lap. Able combed the boy's hair with his fingers, massaging his scalp until he felt comfortable and eventually drifted off to a contented sleep. Able waited until everyone left from the house and then carried Logan with him to his own house. No one would ever be the wiser and he would raise him there as his child.

For years from the time he took Logan in at seven years old, Able trained him in the art of self-defense and self-preservation. He taught him how to silently stalk prey in the open and in crowded areas in which staying concealed was a cinch. He showed him how to fight close hand-to-hand style as well as how to repel attacks. He gave him increasingly powerful weapons to master and was stunned with how quickly he was able to do that very thing. When he was hitting targets up close with untold accuracy, he moved them back and then Logan was able to treat them the same way. Despite the horror of doing so, he then moved Logan to moving targets in the form of small rabbits, squirrels, and similar beings. All along the way he had educated him at home, away from prying eyes and curious minds. He had given him the knowledge he needed about who and what was good or bad and enforced the idea that the bad people who did the bad things needed to be taught a lesson. He had reinforced the idea with human-shaped targets and made him hit them in vital spots like the heart, heard, liver, chest, neck, and gut.

It was only after they had been together for seven years and there was nothing left for Able to teach Logan that he took him into a room he had never entered and sat him down at a large oak table with three uncomfortable metal chairs sitting around it, waiting for a back or butt to destroy. Scattered over the entirety of the table's surface were papers that had numbers in columns and dollar signs. Each of them contained the names of a man at the top that Logan didn't know, and as far as he was concerned, he wasn't supposed to. Able took his own seat and motioned toward the documents making a mess of the oak slab.

"Logan, this is the financial records of a man named Dusty Sardis. He is a wealthy man with no end to his money flow. The problem is, he has not been getting that money legally."

"What do you mean?" asked the fourteen year old with confusion etched on every inch of his face.

"There is another really rich man who does make his money legally, but the first man steals it from him and that's how he got rich in the first place."

"Okay," said Logan. "The first man steals the second man's money and uses it to become rich. That's wrong though."

"Yes, and that's why we are going to teach him and his family a lesson. We leave women and children alone, but the man and his son are fair game," said Able seriously while writing something on a piece of paper. He slid the paper across the table and Logan read it.

"This is an address? Is it the one for the man?" asked Logan.

"Yes, this is his address. His name is Dustin, or Dusty to his friends, Sardis. He will be at home alone tomorrow night from 9:00 to somewhere around 11:00. That gives you two hours to get it done. This is what it has all been building to, son."

"I don't quite understand what you're saying, Able," said Logan.

"I am saying exactly what you think I am, son. I want you to kill Dusty and his son, Brady, and then we will take whatever we can find in the safe inside the house."

"Doesn't that make us as bad as them, Able?" asked Logan who was scouring the papers on the desk as he spoke. His eyes lit up when he came across one that said the man's worth was somewhere around one billion dollars.

"No, we just call that the price of business, son. We rid the world of bad men and pay ourselves with the money they used to become bad."

"Who is the man Dusty stole from?"

"Well, he is a media mogul, uh bigwig, named Samuel Everhart who is worth twenty-five billion dollars."

"You really think Dusty deserves to die for stealing money?" asked Logan.

"Are you asking me what I said instead of doing what I told you?" asked Able, clearly frustrated with the direction the conversation had taken.

"It's just that there are so many other things that people do that make them bad. Why do we want to start with a guy who stole money?"

"We start there because killing rich assholes can make us rich!" said Able in a raised voice. "That's why we take what they leave behind."

"Fine, I was just asking. So, when do we leave?"

"Tomorrow night at 8:00. You have from now until the time I say we are going to study the man, his blueprints for his house, the satellite of the surrounding area, and the documents about his finances. You need a plan on where you will do it from, how long it will take, and where I will need to be waiting to take the safe's contents."

"Okay, then I will need some time," said Logan.

"The room is yours," said Able as he rose, kicked his chair back under the table, and the left the room, slamming the door in his wake.

When the time came for them to leave for their destination, Logan had told Able exactly what the plan was. He was going to lie down on the ridge to the north of the house that had a direct line of sight into a large bay window that didn't actually look out onto a bay or anything else interesting. It was big enough that he could sight them both if they were in the same room without needing to move to a new location. If they were in different rooms, the plan was to wait until Dusty came past the big window and then follow Brady with the scope until he had a clear shot. If he could not get one, then he would move to a new spot and rotate until he got what he needed. He told Able in no uncertain terms that if Brady did not die, he wasn't going to be too concerned. The target in his mind was Dusty. He told Able to wait at the end of the short driveway that led to the modest house. When it was time, he would shine a flashlight briefly into the air.

When they arrived to the property, Able parked in a spot hidden by some trees and where no light from the street penetrated. Logan picked up his rifle and clambered through some wooded landscape and made his way to his post. Able walked to the end of the walk where Logan had told him to be and waited until he was signaled. He pulled out his cell phone and played games on it while Logan went to do the dirty work. He could only hope the boy had been trained well enough and wouldn't become scared when it came to actually taking a human life. He wondered what the boy would say when he learned that his second target was younger than himself. He would definitely have a word or two to say about it. He wasn't shy about speaking his mind.

Logan was on the rise and staring through the scope of the weapon into the intricately decorated home. Despite the man's wealth (according to Able no one was allowed to know he was rich since his job as an accountant would never support such financial standing), he owned a home that most Americans could afford if they worked forty hours, and he had all the furnishings that someone would expect to see in a living room: a large television, a sofa, a recliner, a rocking chair, coffee table, bookshelves. Some of the items appeared to be worth more than average, but no one was going to ask the price of everything in your home once you bought it. They might tell you how nice it looked if you were lucky.

The longer he looked, the more Logan became convinced that perhaps nobody was even home. Not a soul had walked in sight of his scope and he was beginning to grow impatient. Something his training had never prepared him for was waiting for a target to be in range. He was breathing slowly and steadily when the shadow crept across the floor. He saw the silhouette grow and then the man stood before him, the same one from the pictures he had seen while searching through the documents. This was the man he was here to kill, and this was the time to do it.

Able was watching the traffic to make sure that a car passing by would not suspect him of being in the wrong for anything. It was a busier area than he expected, but he was not surprised that Dusty owned the largest lot on the street. Each car that went by ignored him as if he belonged there, and he took that as a good sign. He looked up onto the ridge, only able to see Logan because he knew exactly where to look. He could see him adjusting the weapon. He understood that the deed was about to be done.

Logan had the weapon set to perfection. He calmly placed his index finger of his right hand on the smooth metal trigger and caressed it. When Dusty's head came all the way into the room, followed by his large body, Logan placed the crosshairs over his head. He read his settings to make sure they didn't need further adjusting and then he pressed the trigger, slowly at first, and then when it was perfect timing, with all the power his finger could produce. There was a small click as the trigger snapped, a louder burst as the bullet ejected, and then the glass shattered only in the shape of a round hole and the projectile entered the man's forehead before he even knew he was in the room. The jet of blood from the back of his head told Logan the shell had gone through. Dusty fell to the ground, lifeless. Logan waited with a little more patience and then a second shadow approached. Appearing from it was a boy not even his own age. He was at least three years younger and his heart skipped a beat. What had Able sent him to do? He couldn't refuse if the moment presented itself. He had made that promise. Anger rising in him, he again placed the crosshairs over his target's head and pulled the trigger. Brady died with the same jet of blood and the same quickness. The job was done. At least his part of it was.

Logan reached into his pocket and retrieved an LED flashlight that he pressed the bottom of to engage the lighting mechanism. He pointed it at the sky for three seconds, waving it to be absolutely certain Able would see it. Not caring about the outcome of his gesture, he placed the light back into his pocket and walked back to the car to replace the rifle in the trunk where it belonged. He was stunned to see Able standing there, seemingly waiting for him. He looked at him confused.

"You ain't quite done yet, son," said Able.

"What? What else do I need to do?" asked Logan.

"I never taught you this because I didn't think it would be necessary. I still don't know if it is. When you shoot from as close as you did into the body of a person with that high caliber, you might leave a through-and-through wound. If that's true, then you cannot leave here without getting the casings. If you leave them behind, there is a chance we can be tracked using them."

"You want me to go in there and look for casings?" asked Logan in order to simply clarify Able's expectations.

"Exactly," said Able.

Together they walked to the door of the house unseen. Able picked the lock and they entered the same room where Logan had just ended the lives of two people. The bodies were almost on top of one another. The wounds to the heads could not have been better placed if they had been scripted by a movie screenwriter. Logan could see the holes in the wall where both bullets had come out of the body and entered the plaster. They were not all that deep but he could not dig them out with his bare hands.

Having thought ahead, Able tossed him a pair of pliers before walking to other parts of the house to locate the safe. While he was doing that, Logan removed the shells from the wall and placed them in his jacket pocket. Able came back out with a safe on a blanket being dragged across the wood floor. Silently, Able left for a minute to grab a hand truck and came back and loaded up the safe. They went to the car and struggled to put the box into the trunk. When they had succeeded, they drove away and headed back to the house they shared a good distance away.

Once there, Able opened the safe with some difficulty and they counted the money inside: $200,000. A far cry from what was expected given the man's worth, but a good haul since it was just a simple safe. Able laid the money out and divided it, placing it into two piles on the kitchen table.

"This one is mine," he said, pointing to one stack. "This one is yours, but you are never going to touch this money until you leave home. This is what you will build your life with when you are out on your own."

"That better be half-half," Logan said seriously. "You didn't do anything to earn that money other than setting up the job."

"Like every job you do for me, the pay will be 75% for you and 25% for me. I am already set for life. I did the same shit for my dad when I was little."

From that moment on, there was one job per month. Some of them were local in California, and others required them to travel to cities like New York, Boston, Las Vegas, Chicago, and others. They had obtained over five million dollar by the time Logan was eighteen years old, and 75% was to go to Logan as soon as he chose to leave. He had been tasked with killing every kind of bad man from money launders like Dusty Sardis to killers who had gotten away with it for years. He had taken out politicians seen as corrupt who had done shady things for money under the table and bankers who were skimming off the bank's overall profit. He had perfected the art of using a rifle at various ranges on human targets and had done so on all ages of them. His youngest was and forever would be Brady Sardis. He had never forgiven Able for that job, even if he never actually said anything to him about it.

Working a menial job as a waiter at a run-down fast food restaurant was not Logan's ideal future plans, but there was no way he could, at eighteen years old, pretend that he had life figured out and he definitely couldn't let anyone know that he had millions of dollars put away from killing people for the last four years. He had to act like his life was the same as that of any other person his age. He didn't go to college, primarily because he couldn't since he didn't have school records, but he had achieved an education that would dwarf that of many college educated people he had met, especially the assholes who sat in his section at work on weekends.

He spent his off time going to the gun range to hone his skills with the rifle. He didn't use the actual rifle he did on jobs while at the range, but one similar enough that he could account for the improvements and apply them to the real rifle. There was no way to hide how good he was and he was seen by a lot of people in a busy city like Ebbens. He was rarely the only person his own age firing rounds into a target, but he was never the only person period. The closest he had ever come to that was when a group of local NAVY vets was shooting and there were only six of them. They had rented the place out and he didn't know that until he walked in. They had let him stay and shoot with them, impressed at his prowess and abilities.

Today there was a large group and he was testing distance on the new open field range. There were four other people using it since it only had five open slots. He pulled out his rifle and set it up. The man next to him, dressed in a silk suit of all things, smiled at him before busying himself with his own tasks. Logan, who was wearing ratty blue jeans and a black t-shirt with several extra holes, knelt down all the way to his stomach and read the sight on the scope. He played with the settings until they were just right and then pulled the trigger and put a massive hole right in the center of his torso-shaped target.

He slapped the reel on his scope and it spun freely. He loosened the bolt holding it in place and it fell to the ground like a bag of rocks in water. He picked up the rifle and the mount, moved them both backward and then set them both up again in a firing position. By this time, the man next to him was no longer doing his own thing. He was watching Logan as if he himself were a hawk and the boy next to him his next meal. Logan had finally gotten everything set and knelt back to his crouch on his stomach. He played with the reel he had moved freely and then felt confident with the new settings. When he knew it was all exactly as it should be, he placed his finger on the trigger and pressed. When it was all the way depressed, the bullet jumped from the barrel and plowed into the target at exactly the same spot as the initial one. There was not as much as a fiber of paper there now that was not there before the shot was fired.

The man next to him in the nice suit approached him when he had finished and was heading away from the range. He didn't know what to say to him so he just watched him and waited for the words to come. He was too impressed to express the feelings he was actually trying to. When the words came, he didn't care how they sounded. He only cared that they got through the ears of the kid and he internalized them and agreed to meet with him.

"Hi, I'm Garrett Holder. I was watching you out there today. You have quite a talent with that thing," he said, pointing to the rifle case that Logan was holding up under his hand as it balanced on the floor.

"Oh, thanks," said Logan. "I'm Logan. I have quite a bit of experience with it."

"I can tell," he said. "I don't mean to sound forward but would you like to go to lunch with me so we can talk about a proposal for a job?"

"Hmm, I guess that would be okay. Do you mean now?" asked Logan.

"Yeah, sure. There is a steakhouse around the corner. We can walk over there as soon as you finish up here."

"I'm ready when you are," said Logan.

Seated at a four-person table in the quaint little steak restaurant, the two of them looked at menus and tried to decide on what was both going to be good to eat but also would not cost a fortune. Logan still had to put up the front that he was like everyone else. There was a lot to choose from and Logan chose a simple filet. The suited man ordered a New York strip. While they waited for the meals to arrive, they chatted with one another.

"Alright, now that we are out of earshot other people, I can talk more openly about my job offer."

"Um, could you maybe tell me who you are first?" asked Logan.

"Sure," said the man. "I am an agent for the Central Intelligence Agency. I am here on vacation actually. I work in Washington, DC, and the job I want to offer you is what we like to call a cleaner."

"I have heard that term, but only from my dad. He said the FBI and CIA use cleaners to take out targets who pose a threat to their operations or to what he called national security or something else he called democracy."

"Your dad sounds like a pretty smart guy. That is exactly what we use them to do. The actual title for someone like you would be a paid hitman or assassin."

"I see. I was taught that they are only to be used when people have done something really bad."

"You can trust me. We would never ask you to do anything to anyone who did not deserve it." Holder looked at him to make sure he was getting it. "It might be a world leader, a politician, or just a person with a dangerous plan. Either way, we would only call on you when they truly did something awful."

"I would love to work for you. How do I accept the job officially?" asked Logan.

"You can come back with me to DC and meet my superiors. I explain your qualifications, they test you, train you where and how you need it, and then you are at our beck and call."

"Okay. When do you go back?" asked Logan, sure that he wanted to do this. He had enough experience with the kinds of tasks the CIA would have for him, so why not get paid legally for completing such jobs?

"I can be ready to go back as soon as tomorrow afternoon. If you want to go with me at that time, just let me know." Holder stared at him, again seeing how the news was playing in the young man's mind. He was happy to see that it was making an impact and the kid obviously wanted to do the job since it suited something in him.

When the food came, Holder and Logan continued talking about the job, the kinds of work he would be doing, the cover he could use in his employment with the agency, and how and where Logan would live in the DC area. He took it all in, never even considering telling his dad what he was going to be doing. The arrangement had always been that the moment he stepped out to live on his own, the tether between them had to be severed. The relationship was still there, but Logan had to be cautious about returning and communicating with him in any way. No one had ever asked questions about the missing Aster child, and nobody ever came looking, but that did not mean that curiosity did not still play a major part in the minds of a lot of people in Ebbens.

When the meeting concluded, Holder and Logan went their separate ways with the established plan to meet at the airport the following day at 11:00. Logan went down Suffolk Street and in the direction of his small rent-by-week apartment that he had gotten only because of a generous down payment and no commitment from Logan for any particular amount of time.

He slept well that night and met Holder at the airport the following day as planned. They hopped on a chartered flight and arrived in DC a little over four hours later. Logan stepped off into a city he had been to before, but he could not let on that he was familiar with anything. He had told Holder it would be all-new to him. He looked around the city he knew, but was prepared for a future he definitely didn't.

For four years he worked as a cleaner for the agency, but at the same time he was used by the FBI and several foreign governments to eliminate what they called threats to them. It was the final job that made him decide the time was right to pack up his things and move on to a different life. He liked being paid for doing what he was good at, but the demand was a lot. They asked him to take care of people they said, not proved, were dangerous. He had completed far too many jobs for them that he was unsure of to take another one that had him questioning the validity. When he was told where he was going and who was going to be the target, he didn't immediately jump at the opportunity to be a part of the job. He had begun to take that as a sign that the job was less suitable. He sat at the table in the War Room listening to the discussion with Director Vance Lafferty with open ears despite the feelings he was holding in about it.

"Aster, this is one of the biggest jobs we will ever ask you to be a part of. With the election upcoming in Bursahi, the leading candidate will send them country into chaos and implement communism and kill at will to establish himself as the unfettered leader. His name is Rakasa Grunduma, and he has to be executed before the night prior to the elections. If he lasts longer than that, he will be too dangerous and protected to go after."

"When does this need to be done, then? With the time difference from here to there, it would be the following day there before here. I need some kind of timetable before I can go through with this."

"You have 72 hours to complete the job. You leave in two hours. Your flight lands six hours outside of Nahrasi, the capital city. You have to find your own way to the capital and do the job your way."

Once in Nahrasi, 65 long hours later due to a plethora of delays, Logan set himself up on the top of a residential building across the street from the hotel where Grunduma was staying. He put the rifle on its mount and watched the door for several more hours, knowing his deadline was approaching with rapidity. When the door finally opened and four guards walked out in a circle around him, he knew the time had come. He placed the short man in his crosshairs the way he had grown so fond of doing to people all over the world. No one was expecting anything, and when Logan heard that popping sound that said the case was discharged, he gave a small smile. He saw through the scope as the man's head exploded in a tidal wave of red. Shooting down on a target from such an elevated position made the impact greater. Instead of simply entering the skull, it ripped it apart as it did so. He packed his rifle and disappeared into the wind as he had done countless times before. Another job completed, but he wasn't sure he had done the right thing. It was a feeling he hated but it came with a great paycheck so he had also taught himself to ignore it.

Upon his arrival back at Langley, he went directly to the office of the director, Lafferty, and resigned his position. He walked away from the job and decided to go out on his own. He thought he could do better on his own, but it was so much more than that. He didn't need or want the money that would come with it, but this way he could choose his jobs more carefully, vet them before completing them. He left Langley for the final time and adopted a nickname that befit his skillset and ability to vanish when a job was complete: The Vapor. As he walked away, he could hear the news reports that Bursahi elections were complete and the country was rioting and there was death in all corners. He heard one report that made him certain he was doing the right thing. The words stuck with him thereafter: "If only Grunduma had been elected instead of assassinated, this country would be looking at true democracy. It was always more likely than not that Shurruma would be a chaotic choice as he was the one the people had adamantly stated they did not want in power."

CHAPTER TWO

Branding himself as The Vapor was good for business among a select few people who understood what it was that he was attempting to accomplish, but it was not lucrative enough to keep him busy all the time. He had only been using word-of-mouth to obtain customers, though he knew there were other ways that people used to market themselves and their businesses. He took to advertising in magazines and online. His reputation took off and it was not long before his schedule was so full that there was not even an open moment in his day.

As the job began to consume so much of his time, he brought in enough money to live anywhere he wanted and travel anywhere he was needed. It was seldom that he was required to journey overseas, but he loved when it happened. Some of his best and favorite jobs came when he was outside of the United States. He enjoyed both the cultural aspect as well as the occasional sightseeing he could do while in exotic locales. He was needed in the United States more than he would like, but there were a few cities that he loved being in and one of those was Washington, DC.

He had been making camp in the little apartment he rented in New York City when his phone beeped and he looked at the message with curiosity. It was short and to the point. It contained a name, location, fee, and deadline. The man's name was Harold Finnigan and he was in DC. The message said the client was willing to pay him the handsome fee of $100,000 but the job needed to be completed in forty-eight hours or less with confirmation of the kill. The only thing he didn't like about this kind of job was that he had to be close to the target so he could photograph the kill as proof of the completion.

He sat down at his computer and opened the internet. He searched for Harold Finnigan to learn a little about his target. What he learned was disheartening. The man was definitely not worth the usual fee he charged, so it made sudden sense that he was offered less right off the bat. His advertisement did say he was willing to consider offers if the client thought the target was not worth the usual amount. This was undoubtedly among the cases that fit the profile.

Finnigan had done nothing more than apparently sleeping with the wife of a renowned NBA basketball player when he was in California watching a game. It had made big news locally, but not beyond that. Unfortunately, Finnigan was a politician, low-level though he may have been, and that meant the media coverage and accompanying investigation would be intense and constant. Logan was going to have to take extreme care not to leave behind any kind of evidence that could link him to the execution. He was going to need to think long about how to do it since there would be security, and it would not be easy to get in or out of any place, especially the home of a politician, without being seen. The issue was keeping from being identified, more than it was keeping from being seen.

He learned all he could from the internet about his target so he moved on to researching the area in which Finnigan lived. His home was in an affluent section of the city known simply as Capitol Hill. The building he lived in alone with his little dog was called 425 Mass Apartments and it was a truly luxurious building. Given the ready availability of information on the internet, Logan was able to easily discover not only the building, but the exact apartment in which the man made his home. He lived in a two bedroom and two bath loft style apartment that had a total of over fifteen hundred square feet of space. Looking at the layout of the room, Logan was able to determine a plan of action for when he arrived.

He took out one of the many credit cards he possessed with a random, fake name on it, and booked a flight into Dulles for the next afternoon. He planned to drive from Dulles into the city in a rented car and park several blocks away from the complex. He would walk down the street, the same as anyone who lived or belonged in the area, and then enter the building with another person, or perhaps a group if all went well. His plan B was to call 9-1-1 and report a fake emergency and enter with them, but that was asking for trouble if it went south. Once inside the building, he would ascend the stairs to the seventh floor and then enter the room he was destined for. In his head it all sounded so simple. The more he thought about it, the more it coursed through his brain just how much could potentially go wrong.

The flight from New York to DC was short and uneventful. Logan got to the airport and was whisked through the process of getting baggage and exiting the building quickly. He grabbed a meal at his favorite local spot, a small diner not far from the White House from which he could see all of the famous structures in the city. He wanted to wait until it got dark before moving in on the target, but his patience was running thin. He had called the office where the man worked to check on his whereabouts, and as of a half an hour ago, he was still sitting at his desk, busy. The secretary mentioned that he had meetings planned until 8:00 meaning he would leave the office around 9:00.

Not wanting to sit around idle until it was time to act, Logan went to the park and sat on a bench there just watching all of the people. He couldn't help but imagine that any of them could be his target at any time for the right price. He even caught himself giving some of them a value that he might act for. Of course, knowing nothing about why they might be targeted made that a pointless endeavor. He smiled at the kids playing on the equipment designed for such things. When he was young, his daily fun had come from hunting small animals or shooting a target on the man-made range on his adoptive father's property.

He was engrossed in watching a young couple intently when a woman with nothing remarkable about her features or presence sat down clumsily next to him on the old wood bench that was in need of some repair. She was silent and keeping a close eye of her own on a little teacup poodle that was obviously not her own. She was about as interested in the dog as the average person is about getting surgery. She glanced at Logan and smiled quickly, cutting it off before it got uncomfortable for either of them.

"Hi," said Logan, catching her glance and making her blush.

"Hi," said the woman. "I wasn't staring, I swear."

"It's fine if you were," said Logan. "I am not going to fault a pretty woman for looking."

"You think I'm pretty?" asked the woman with a chuckle.

"Well, I am not in the habit of telling people they are ugly. Seems a bit mean," he said seriously. He was putting on display the fact that he had been raised with nearly zero humor to speak of and the result was that he didn't really understand how to use it, when it was appropriate, or when someone else was using it.

The woman looked at him in confusion, but she didn't know how to respond to him. He seemed to be genuinely kind, but that answer was weird and it was not exactly the kind of thing, or even in the realm, of what she was expecting.

"My name is Janet," was all she could come up with and it seemed like the right thing since he responded to that with more of a smile, though it was kind of a sideways one.

"Hi, Janet. I'm Logan," he said, forgetting for the briefest second that he not only was there under an assumed name and didn't have a single thing with that name on it, but also that he was not supposed to reveal his true name to anyone for his and their safety. There was no way to put the cat back in the bag once it was out, so he was stuck being his real self with this woman, whoever she was.

"Nice to meet you, Logan," Janet said politely. "So, what brings you out here today?"

"I am in town for work," Logan said simply. "I won't be here long. I do business all over the country."

"What kind of business are you in?" asked Janet, carrying the conversation to what would be easy topics for a normal person.

"Finance, mostly. I work with a lot of wealthy people and they pay me. I guess the same could be said for any job though."

"It sounds nice. I guess it would be better if working for rich people guaranteed we would be rich too," said Janet with that same chuckle.

"Oh, I'll never get rich." He was serious again, despite her attempt to lighten him up.

"Me either, so I guess we found something we have in common." She said this while not looking at him, but watching the dog she had accompanied. He was now playing with a group of kids around the swings. If being partially buried for laughs could be considered playing.

"Is he yours?" asked Logan, pointing to the animal being goofily tormented by youth.

"Mine? Good god, no. He belongs to a friend of mine, but I take him to the park in the afternoons while she is working. If she would pay me, maybe I could get rich." She was shocked when she heard a slight giggle from next to her. She wasn't sure it was Logan, but convinced it was, she didn't want to be disappointed if it wasn't so she didn't check.

The two of them continued talking and bonding, though Logan had no intentions of that happening. Able had always told him that even with the job he was in the habit of doing, the day would come when he would find a woman and have to make the choice to continue the life or be domestic and put that life on hold. The other option was total honesty and there was no way he was going to tell anyone what he did for a living.

When the time came for her to leave and return the pet she was sitting for, they had talked for over an hour and had contact information for one another. Logan could only give her his actual number and it happened to be the same one people used to send him messages about who they wanted killed. She had given him her actual number and they had exchanged text messages to ensure both were being honest. They smiled at one another and then went their separate ways.

When he was walking down the street in the direction of the building where his target resided, he got a message from Janet. He read it while continuing at his normal pace and could not help but smirk, something that was new to him, but he was starting to enjoy. She had invited him out to dinner at a French restaurant the following evening, and he sent a message to her in response agreeing to meet her. He was stunned by his own behavior.

Finally, Logan arrived at his destination and it was busier than he anticipated, and that was a great thing. He waited until more than one person at a time was trying to squeeze their way into the entrance and stepped in among them, no one the wiser. He stayed behind a taller man, keeping pace with him until he turned toward the elevator. Logan went right for the stairs, a location no one else in the building was heading. When he reached them, he was not excited about climbing seven landings. The best part of his night was going to be taking the elevator back down when it was all over.

On the floor he was anxious to reach finally, he walked to the door of the apartment he needed with purpose and anyone who saw him would never doubt he belonged there. They may become curious if they saw him entering the apartment of a politician who was known to live there. He made a quick point of not being noticed doing so, and for the benefit of the straggling family in the hallway, he made a show of tying his shoe and stood up only when they had opened their own door and gone inside. They had never so much as acknowledged his presence.

The apartment door was too easy to pick and Logan smiled as he did it. Literally anyone could come inside this room if they had ever tried to open a lock of any kind by mischievous means. When it popped open, he was taken aback by the spacious nature of the layout. When he had studied it online, he had seen the size in numerical form, but to see it actually laid out there was enough space to make a couple of full-size apartments. For that matter, he had been in houses with less square footage. He crept in and shut the door gingerly behind him to avoid making any noise. He locked the door back and then got to work.

It was finally 9:00 when he realized that he had been busy for quite some time. He had wiped everything off that he may have touched, including the door. He would worry about the outside after he left. He made sure there were no prints of any kind that would alert Finnigan to the presence of another person. He had a lot of spots he could lie-in-wait, but the best option was crouched down behind the island in the kitchen. Over the course of his time as a hitman, he had learned to be patient in a way he had never dreamed possible. Even if it took another day for Finnigan to return, he would be crouched down waiting for him to walk through the door. Luckily, it only took a half an hour.

From his vantage point, Logan heard the door open with all of the subtlety of a crashing freight train. It slammed hard against the wall and then once again as it was latched in place. He could hear both shoes flying into the floor from an elevated position. The man was stomping through the house, careless of the neighbors next door, nearby, or beneath him. The next sound was the bathroom door operating much the same way. For a short second, Logan thought the man might be angry enough to put up a fight and make it a challenge for him. Then he remembered seeing images online of a man big enough to need a double-door on his vehicle. The worst he would be is hard for Logan to get his hands all the way around. That's why he liked to use the garrote. It had a wire that was more than long enough, and he didn't have to touch it since he could pull using the handles on either end.

Finnigan came out of the bathroom wearing only his boxers and sluggishly walked over to the kitchen and opened the refrigerator. Logan could hear a bottle of some kind of carbonated beverage being popped open, and then footsteps heading in his direction. When he saw the white sock appear around the edge, he sprang into action. Like a bolt of lightning he struck, flipping one end of the weapon to his open right hand from his left and then deftly placing it around the neck of the large man. As he squeezed, he could tell there was not as much force being put on the vital areas as there would be for a skinny person. He pulled harder, his inhuman strength coming into play at the right time. His muscles bulged and his veins popped, but he pulled back with all his might, finally cutting deep into the flesh.

The fat man struggled mightily, kicking with flailing legs and then dropping to his knees. Logan went with him without missing a beat. Finnigan threw his head from side to side and made no progress. His face was turning blue and rivulets of blood were oozing from the wound in his neck. Finnigan was gasping silently as the airflow was cut off and nothing was reaching his lungs. His head drooped to the side after a minute and Logan held on for a minute more. When he was sure the target was deceased, he released the grip and let the body drop to the floor completely and unceremoniously.

When he stood up and removed his leather gloves, he took out his phone and opened the messaging app he used for his services. He clicked the little image of a camera and it opened on his screen. He clicked the icon to capture the image and then pressed the button to send it to the client. Within seconds he had a notification from his banking app that $100,000 had been deposited. He pocketed the phone and the weapon and left the apartment, wiping the door on his way out. It would not be long before he was found, and it was unfortunate that whoever found him would enter through an unlocked door. That was something he simply couldn't do anything about.

He glared at the door leading to the stairs. No way was he going to use those again. He walked over to the elevator, pressed the button for the lobby, and enjoyed the short ride. When it reached the bottom, he walked out as if he was just leaving the building for a quick second, no one the wiser yet again, and exited, free of consequence. He had that same feeling he often got after a job: the balance was restored. Another evil entity would never cause trouble again. Some people might call him evil, but he saw it another way: he did what others would not to rid the world of people it didn't want or need.

The following day, when Logan had originally planned to leave and go back to New York, he instead found himself enjoying a nice French meal with Janet at a place called Les Desales, not far from his hunting ground the previous night. Logan enjoyed the Cajun Mahi Mahi while Janet chowed down on a simple beef burger that was as delectable as any she had ever tasted.

They spent the whole meal talking, deepening the bond that was created mere hours before at the park. There was laughter, mostly from Janet, and they had a good time. When the meal was over, they once again parted ways. This would be the beginning of their time together and not the end. They would be the catalyst to changing one another in unimaginable ways.

CHAPTER THREE

It wasn't long before Logan and Janet decided to marry, though it threw a major wrench in the career plans for Logan. He was working feverishly to hide his life from his wife, and the closer they grew to one another, the more likely it was that she would discover the truth. Logan figured that she had some assumptions about what he did anyway, but when the finances were factored in, there was no way she was naïve enough to believe all of it was coming from legitimate work. He had claimed to work in finance, and the ruse worked since he didn't have to explain anything, but when it came down to how much he made for his vague work content, he could only carry the lie so far without raising more questions that were answered.

When Logan completed a job five years into their marriage and the alert went to his phone, he was not the one to see it. Janet picked it up and all she could do was stare in horror. The message said "for completion, here is the total of $1,000,000. For doing it so quickly, I have added $500,000." She dropped the phone on the floor and Logan came running, assuming something had happened to her. He was happily surprised she was fine when he entered the kitchen.

"What is going on in here? I thought you were hurt!" said Logan.

"Oh, I'm fine," Janet said with fury behind her calmness. "Would you mind explaining this to me?" she asked, reaching down, picking up the phone, and thrusting it into his open hands with the message staring him in the face.

He read it, knowing that there was nothing he could do or say that could possibly make that message make any kind of sense. He understood he was in a hole that digging out of might be impossible. It wouldn't shock him too much if she packed her bags and walked away without a sound.

"It's a confirmation of a job, that's all."

"A job? That paid you 1.5 million dollars? Do you think I was born yesterday?" asked Janet, frustrated and drumming her fingers on the countertop.

"Some jobs pay more than others. That's the way the business world works. If you buy something from the store and then buy the same thing somewhere else, the price likely won't be the same."

"You are justifying this by telling me how supply and demand works? Do you honestly think I don't know that your job isn't exactly what you tell me it is? We don't live in this house because you do honest work all the time."

"I'm just telling you. The next job might pay less, but it is still a paycheck. I don't rely on the amounts of the checks. I rely on how many I can earn at a time. This happened to be a huge one."

"Bullshit, Logan!" screamed Janet. "I'm not gonna ask what it is you do because that isn't my business. What I am gonna ask is why this one is worth so much and what other ones have you done that earn this kind of money?"

"I have done several worth this kind of money. I don't always tell you how much we make, and sometimes I do them and never tell you I did them at all."

"So, you lie to me? You keep secrets from me?"

"No, goddammit! I protect you!" yelled Logan, losing his cool. Not knowing how he could continue, he left the room with Janet staring blankly, wondering what her husband meant by needing to protect her. Not only was she now curious about the nature of his work, but also the people for whom he did these so-called jobs.

The next several jobs were worth much less, but he did them mostly out of a need to wash off the stench of the fight with Janet. He didn't check them out the way he usually did, and when he completed the jobs, he didn't feel the remorse he occasionally felt. He was feeling something he had never felt before in its place and he was not sure one way or another whether he liked it or not. He could sense that he was letting a darker part of himself come to the surface, and he was unsure how it would play out in his personal life. He had been arguing much more with Janet since her little discovery.

The night she told him, in their tenth year of marriage, that she was pregnant, he lost his mind. The marriage was never supposed to happen, but a child was damn sure never supposed to be a part of the equation. He didn't tell her he was happy even once. He didn't act like he cared about the child. She was incredibly happy with the news, but it was more because she knew it would rope him in if she kept it more than her actually wanting it. She also expected that it would calm him down and bring him back to earth emotionally. She got the exact opposite reaction.

When little Anisa was born nine months later, he changed his tune in the best possible ways. He loved and cared about her more than he ever had anything or anyone in his life. He held her every time he was home and took charge of all her needs. Janet went the other way. She resented the child first for driving a wedge between her and Logan, and then because she never did quite bond with her the way she had been told countless times that a baby would. Logan's love for his daughter led him to make a drastic choice that was better for him and her. He had begun to stop caring about Janet at all.

He gave up the life that made him so comfortable while also being the most lucrative thing he would ever do. He didn't want to risk failing a job and not being there for Anisa as she grew. The more she became a little girl, the less Janet cared about what or who she was becoming. The bond didn't exist between them, so it was unlikely she would ever be the one to care for their daughter. When the moment came and he was allowed in by waiver, Logan joined the United States Marine Corps. He was trained as a sniper and enjoyed the thrill of the kill in a completely different way.

The training that had gotten him to where he was both excited and terrified Logan. He had been told a lot while growing up that he would use it as much as he wanted and he could even decide how he went about doing so. He had never once considered that might have meant killing people in the name of the government, not only for one agency, but multiple. The more the war on terror took him around the globe, the more he fell in love with the sound of a gunshot and the impact it made in the chest or head of a deserving individual on the other end. He killed only when told to do so, which was new territory for him, but he had become so good at it that there was never any doubt on who to call on when the need arose to have someone eliminated. That was the word superiors liked: eliminated. It was basically murder, but Logan didn't care one way or another. He was pulling in a steady enough paycheck to take care of the family and still taking the lives of what he thought of as human filth.

On his leave, he would go home only to see Anisa since his relationship with Janet had become more strained than he ever imagined possible. He had not stopped loving her, though he had thought more than once that was the case. He had only grown tired of her mistreatment of their daughter and her awful means of lashing out at anyone who tried to tell her that parenting genuinely sucked. He loved her for reasons that had nothing to do with their child and the love had come long before Anisa was even born. He was absolutely certain that Janet no longer cared for, much less loved, him, and he was okay with that. She wanted to stay around for their daughter's sake, and he was fine with that too.

Before what was to be his final leave, he had to complete a job in Afghanistan that nearly cost him his own life. It was laid out as a simple hit that would require him to be no closer than a few hundred yards from the target. This was a distance he was quite accustomed to since he had become best friends with his rifle and learned how to hit the eye of President Lincoln on a penny with astonishing accuracy from such distances. The plan was for him to perch on the building next door, something he had done many times as a civilian and as a contractor for government agents. When the man exited, he was to execute the man and disappear, earning his nickname of The Vapor. As he vanished, he was to rendezvous with the evac team and head to the safety of the Air Force base there and then fly home for the final time.

After twelve years of doing what he was told and when, this job was looking as easy as any other. It was only when he arrived on the scene to do the task at hand that he recognized a lot of red flags, and eventually the job collapsed around him, giving him an all-new perspective.

When the first hand grabbed his shoulder, he snapped it at the wrist, and a scream reminiscent of a horror movie came from the throat of the man at the end of it. He dropped the hand just in time to absorb a punch to his midsection that caught him off guard and knocked the wind completely out of him. The man stood over him with a mask covering his face, but he was clearly a local. His dark eyes lowered in a way that suggested he was angry about something. With Logan still on the ground, he stomped on to his gut twice in quick succession. Logan had still not fully caught his breath from the last blow and this one made it worse. A third man approached and the two of them reached down, ripped him to a standing position, and dragged him away into the darkness through the nearby market.

He was thrown into a cage like an animal and kept there all day, every day without food until night time and only getting water three times daily in small doses. He began to lose the bulk in his musculature and he grew faint quickly when the heat permeated his cage. He was weak and getting weaker all the time. He was never told anything about why he was there or what they wanted from him, and with each passing day, he understood he was being slowly killed in a horrifying way. He wouldn't exactly starve and he wasn't going to die from thirst, but he was wasting away.

He was taken out one afternoon and dragged with handcuffs on his wrists and a blindfold to a concrete room where he was thrown down onto a concrete bench and then two massive men sat on either side of him. He felt squished and uncomfortable but he wasn't about to attempt to move. As if reading his mind each man took one of his arms and held it tightly, preventing any movement.

The man in the front of the room, a local who never gave his name (and come to think of it, he never knew the name of anyone he met there) spoke with clarity, but in his own language. Logan didn't speak any Persian so he was lost from the start. It was only when another person, a woman with an accent that sounded American or perhaps Canadian, translated that he knew what was happening.

"This is your trial and here we will decide if you are guilty or innocent. Guilt means we put you to death since the penalty for your crimes is death by stoning," said the woman in perfect English.

"I have done nothing wrong," said Logan. "You have kept me locked up here for two years, and I don't understand why."

The woman he could not see translated the words to the leader and then turned to Logan to give him the reply. She was cold with her words, speaking of death and cruelty as easily as some people discussed their love of puppies.

"You are accused of the crime of murder and attempted murder," said the woman. "You were caught with weapons of death used by the United States in the place an important man was staying at the time."

"I am in the military," pleaded Logan. "Of course I had weapons from America."

"This was no weapon used by low-level soldiers," said the woman. "This was a weapon used to kill, and from a great distance."

"It was to protect myself from the dangers here, that's all."

"You are lying," she said. "We were told to expect you and that you were here to kill a prominent man. When you arrived, we knew the information was valid."

"It is my job. I was just doing my job, the same as you are now."

"No, that is not good enough. You were here to kill, and that is punishable by death. We know you were here for that purpose because we were told you were coming."

"That is attempted murder, so who I am accused of killing? You also said I was being charged with murder," said Logan.

"There are many men you have killed, and we are going to be the judge of your crimes. We know what you have done, but we want to hear why you killed good men for America's corrupt leaders."

"Good men? Is that really who you think I killed? They were criminals, murderers, extortionists, warlords, drug lords. The world is better without those people in it," said Logan seriously. He tried to peer through the thick black cloth covering his eyes, but to no avail. He still couldn't move his arms or body due to the tree-sized men holding on to him.

"They are not bad because you say so. They are good men who did what they had to do to survive. The same thing you claim to be doing in killing them," said the woman. She was getting harsher with her words, and Logan began to wonder if that was because of her own personality or if she was matching an intensity being exhibited in the man's voice.

"They are bad men because those things are wrong and the people who do them are bad. I did what I had to, yes, but it was also because it was the right thing to do."

"You are not the judge of right and wrong. Only Allah can judge man, and he chose me and this council to be his voice. We judge the men you killed to be doing the necessary thing to survive, but you have been judged to be wrong, an evil man."

The banter went back and forth for several more minutes and then the leader was ready to pronounce judgment and sentencing. Logan was nervous and unsure of what was going to happen. He had spent two years being beaten, tortured, and tormented all in the name of Allah, and today was either going to be the end of that or the end of him.

The leader rose to his full height and stood before the small gathering. The other members of the council who had remained silent on the sides of him, stared in awe. It was like they were looking into the face of a celebrity or a god. His words were law and that meant whatever he said next was not only going to be the law, but it was going to come to pass sooner rather than later. They all hung on his every word.

"After reviewing all of the evidence we have against you and listening to your own testimony about the events for which you are on trial, it is the judgment of this council that you are guilty on all counts and will be executed at the dawning of the day tomorrow. Your execution will be by stoning in a public display in the center of the city."

Logan's heart sank. He didn't know why he had been found guilty or what he was guilty of exactly, but he understood that his life was over in a mere few short hours. He was going to die much younger than he imagined and in a way that no person alive should have to endure. He kept thinking about Anisa and how much he missed her. He wanted so badly to get back to her, and now he never would. He lost all train of thought as he was being dragged back to his lockup.

His mind got busy working while he sat idly in the corner of the box he called home. He knew the schedule of the guards for the most part, but there were so hiccups in his timing. He had tested it throughout the afternoon and evening. He knew exactly how far it was to certain points once outside of the cage, but he wasn't quite sure of how many guards there would be, which ones would be on duty, or where he would go if he made it out alive. Those were the biggest details and also the ones he had to figure out before dawn. The more he thought about them, the more options he came up with in his mind. There was a lot of danger in not choosing the right one the first time, so he began drawing pictures in the dirt with his finger. He had finally, only an hour or two from dawn, come up with the perfect plan. He would have to accomplish it all without a weapon or exit strategy, but those were things he could deal with when it came time.

A half hour before dawn, the cell door was flung open with zero care. It slammed on the metal of the wall and made a sound like dropping a large fork on a cooking pan. Logan pretended to be asleep and then slowly roused, forcing the two guards waiting outside to come in a physically force him to his feet. The first of them was short and strong, so Logan went for his knees, kicking the left one so hard that it bent all the way backward, forcing a cry as the man collapsed to the ground in agony. He swept the leg of the second, taller guard and then reached down and snapped the neck of the first. While he was standing back up, the second guard punched him square in the jaw with a hook that staggered him badly.

Logan recovered and went for the man like he was tackling him and was caught by the collar of his shirt and thrown to the ground. Lying on his stomach, the man dropped with his knee and put it right into Logan's back with an audible crack. Logan was losing the battle he should have easily won, and he was not happy. Not sure what was broken or cracked, he stood and swung several times at the man's face, connecting with each one and knocking the guard to the ground on his ass. He kicked him in the jaw with all of the strength he could muster, which wasn't much with the damage to his back that he could feel every time he raised his leg. The man fell with a thud and then Logan repeated the neck snap and ran as fast as he could to the open door. He was in severe pain and with each step it felt as if he was being hit in the back with a bowling ball.

Once out of the cell, he ran for the open entryway to the hovel where he was being held. He could hear voices coming closer to him and knew that he would not be able to overpower them on his own with the injury to his back. He raced back to the cell and stripped the men of the small firearms and made sure they had full cartridges before moving back to the hallway. He was met there by several guards that he had to shoot in order to escape. With each shot, he worried that either more would come or one would attack in between. He was able to get through all of them before making it to the door. Once outside, he saw the procession of people waiting for him to be walked down the street and buried to his neck. They carried rocks, some big and some small, ready to throw them at his head until he was dead. He shivered at the thought.

Without being seen, something of a specialty of his, he disappeared in the other direction, avoiding the crowd and making his way for the part of town where he could find a phone and perhaps safety. It was as if every person in town was at the execution site. He wasn't sure how many people would be in their shops or anywhere else, but he had to try to find someone to help him. The ache in his back was so excruciating now that he could barely stay up on his feet. When he was a few blocks from the part of town he was heading for, he felt a hand on his shoulder, and his instinct kicked in as he prepared to break the wrist and run.

Logan was met at the airport three days later by his daughter who was now 14 and his wife who actually seemed genuinely pleased to see him. They all hugged one another and left, going home together for the first time in over two years. A lot had changed, but the love of his family was not one of those many things. Logan was glad to be home, but he already missed the life he had come to love as a member of the elite killing force he had been part of for over a decade. He was sitting at home relaxing after his back surgery, recovering and waiting his daughter to come home from school. He heard the knock on the door and then he saw the shadow in the smoked glass of the front door. He was the only one in the house so he had to be the one to answer. He limped over to the door, pulled it open and stared into the face of a terrifying man dressed all in black and holding a gun.

CHAPTER FOUR

The man was intimidating and Logan was not sure what to think about him at first. He was ready to attack if he needed to, but the man put his sidearm away when he saw that Logan, ironically, was no threat to him. He was extremely tall, well over six feet, thin, and built of nothing but muscle. He would have been able to scare monsters. He didn't smile and he also didn't frown. He had some kind of neutral expression on his face that Logan, who was generally quite good at doing so, could not read at all. He started to walk past Logan into the house but was pushed backward with a gentle shove.

"Excuse me, but what the hell do you think you're doing?" asked Logan, staring into the face of the man, who despite his own height of six-three, he had to look up to see completely.

"I'm coming in, if that's okay," said the man coldly and then pushed Logan aside like he was a child.

"Fine, but I am warning you, if you try anything, I will not hesitate to," but he was cut off by the man's gruff reply.

"Shut the fuck up! You're not going to do anything to me."

"Again, who do you think you are? What do you think you're doing?"

"I came to speak with you before someone else tried to snatch you up, so to speak."

"What are you talking about?" asked Logan "Are you talking about some kind of job offer? Because I already have a job."

"That's more or less why I am here, but you don't have a job, we both know that's a fucking lie." The man stared hard at Logan, drumming his fingers against his thigh as he spoke. "You are good at what you do. Yes, I know exactly what it is you do."

"What I do? Care to explain what you mean by that?"

"Simple. You kill people for money. You have killed countless people and amassed a genuine fortune doing it. We need your skills."

"Even if that is true, how the fuck do you know who I am?"

"I know all about your career in the killing game. I have been watching you for a long time."

"Um, I am wondering why you would have been watching me."

"We have a, let's call it a mutual companion. Basically, they told me about you and I kept an eye on your work. Never even seen you miss a shot."

"Okay, so you know the truth about me. So what? Why are you here?"

"My name is Nestor Jacobson. I go by the handle of Komodo within my 'company." He stared at Logan, waiting for some kind of reaction and got nothing. "We are mercenaries, of a sort, and we are looking for someone with a skillset like yours that we can harness and get jobs we wouldn't otherwise get."

"Are you telling me you want to use me to get more work?" asked Logan, confused.

"More or less, yes. If we have a hitman, something we don't have now, then we can seek out jobs of a different sort. We need you, and I am pretty sure you need us too."

"I don't need you. I can go back to doing it independently any time I want. As you said, I made a fortune doing it, and I can just add to that."

"What if I told you that the risk would be minimal, the financial benefit would be more than independence, and you would only work when you wanted?"

"I don't need money, I can work any time I want now, and I don't mind the risks. They come with the territory."

"I don't want to tell you what to do, but at your age in this game, independence has some major drawbacks. Young blood is the way most clients go these days."

"Offer me something that I cannot get independently and I will consider your offer."

"Okay, there is one thing I can offer you above all else: there is no more sole responsibility, for better or worse. We live and die as a unit. If one of us fails, we all do, but we also all share in the successes."

They continued to talk and Logan learned that the man worked for a unit he called The Animal Kingdom. He said that all of the members had codenames or handles of animals, mainly elite hunters, and that they were the best in the world at a particular skill. He had an IT whiz, a weapons specialist, a hand-to-hand combatant, a tracker, and he was a reconnaissance man himself. The only thing they lacked, so he said, was a long-range kill threat. He wanted badly for Logan to be that man. Logan turned him down, but Nestor told him that he would remain in touch and would continue to follow him should he decide to pursue working again.

Jacobson left disappointed in his black Lexus and Logan was left with an empty feeling. He knew he had done the right thing, but he wasn't sure that there were not advantages to being a part of a team that would take a lot of the heat off of him. He had long ago decided though that he was going to work for himself after so long working for the government. He had done all he could or wanted to do for them, and he knew he could do anything he wanted and Anisa would never question it as long as he was there for her.

The door opened and in ran his teenage daughter. She didn't hug him the way she used to when she came home from school. She was long past that since he had started to recover and life had taken a turn for the somewhat normal over the last few weeks. She missed him more than words could say when he was in prison, but as soon as he got home, she adapted to having him back, as resilient kids often do, and then gone about her life as if he had never been gone in the first place. She had grown accustomed to him being away while he was in other countries for weeks or months at a time when he served in the military. Two years to her was just an extended one of those journeys.

"Hey, kiddo. Welcome home," he said as she rummaged through the refrigerator looking for something to eat as a snack.

"Hey, daddy," came the automatic reply. "Do we have anything sweet?"

"Nope, I need to go shopping. There are some chips in the cabinet or some ice cream in the freezer."

"Ice cream is sweet, genius," she said playfully. "Anyway, go shopping. Like, now. We need some sweets."

"I cannot keep this awesome physique if I buy I bunch of sweets," he said, looking down at the belly he had developed from a lack of mobility, and his scrawny arms that were the result of being nearly starved for two years.

"Yeah, don't wanna mess that up, do we?"

"Are you being sarcastic with me?"

"Nope, don't even know what the word means, you loser," she said with a chuckle.

"You better be nice to me. One day, I will be gone and all you will have are these mean jokes to remember me with."

"Oh trust me, I plan to remember them. It's not all I have. I have sarcastic comments too."

"Yeah, those too," said Logan.

She sat in the living room floor eating ice cream and watching a television show while Logan rested in his recliner. They spoke now and again, but mostly it was silence for the two of them, and they both enjoyed every second of it. The times like these were becoming fewer and neither would admit that they were going to miss it when it was gone.

The door opened again and Janet stormed in and threw it closed like a tornado of anger. She stomped across the floor toward the kitchen and threw her purse at the sofa along the way.

"Why is that girl such a royal bitch? I swear to god!" She was talking about one of her coworkers, a young girl named Franny Goldwater, and she was not a royal bitch. Janet just literally hated her. Everything about her.

"Hi, sweetie. Bad day?" asked Logan with a smirk as he looked at his daughter's reddening face.

"Very funny, asshole," she said to Logan. She was in the kitchen and then she spoke again. "Jesus, Anisa. Can't you clean up your goddamn mess when you eat something? There is ice cream on the counter, a spoon on the table, and the freezer isn't even closed all the way."

"She will take care of it, Jan. Let her finish."

"Oh, of course, daddy to the rescue. Little girl can't do any wrong. Forget it. I will clean it myself. It's probably what the little brat wanted anyway."

"Cool it, Jan. Now," said Logan. "I have already had enough of this attitude. You have been home five minutes and already ruined two hours of a good time."

"Oh, sorry," she said sarcastically with an evil laugh. "Did I throw a wrench in bonding time? God forgive me!"

Logan, through no fault of his own, started thinking about the man who had been in the house earlier in the day. As twisted an idea as it was, it would help him to blow off steam and deal with the day-to-day rigors of his wife's hatred for their only child. He could still make great money if the figures Nestor had told him were accurate, and he would only be home when he wanted to be. He knew that meant they would be alone together more often and it worried him, but Janet was adult enough not to kill Anisa out of spite. He just wished the man had left some way for him to get in contact, and not just said that he would be in touch.

After another fight between Janet and Anisa about a dirty room, Logan had intervened and then gone to bed pissed off. He didn't know how to get to the heart of what was upsetting Janet so much about Anisa, but he couldn't take the arguing any longer. He lay in his bed with his mind on a dozen things unrelated to family and each of them was better for his mental health. He fell asleep to the sound or rain drumming on the roof.

When he woke the next morning, Anisa was already at school and Janet had left for work. He was watching the news when his doorbell rang. He wasn't expecting anyone, and when he answered it, he was shocked to see Nestor standing there once again. This time, he was wearing a blue silk suit and white shirt with a red tie. He still had that same expression Logan could not read.

This time, they talked solely about the decision Logan had made the night before while trying to fall asleep angry. Nestor was happy to hear that Logan had chosen the life of The Animal Kingdom over being an independent operator. He wouldn't admit to himself or Logan that it had a lot to do with the fact that Logan had taken clientele from them with his elite skills and it had ultimately cost them a lot of money. If he worked for them, then the same clients would come crawling back looking to use their services. They agreed to meet the following day at noon at the headquarters of the Animal Kingdom.

It was a little like looking for a back-alley restaurant, but Logan was finally able to shamble down the correct street and locate the red brick building Nestor had told him to look for when he arrived there. The door was thick metal and blue. He knocked three times, as instructed and when the slide opened and he saw eyes, he prepared to give the passphrase to enter but the person behind the door never asked him for it. The door opened to reveal a large open room with nothing in it except the man who had opened it for him. He was fat, short, and ugly enough that a few moms would have asked for him to be put back in. Logan walked past him without even acknowledging him. He didn't know where to go so he stopped when he came to a row of offices.

As if he had some kind of radar, Nestor came out of one of the doors and approached Logan. He still wore that same expression. He took Logan's hand and shook it robotically. It was something both of them had done at least a million times in their lives. He led him silently into the same door he had exited from and shut the door slowly behind him. Nestor handed Logan a thick contract to read and sign, of which he read every word and then put his signature in all of the required spots. Unthinkingly, he placed the pen in his pants pocket in case he needed it again. The encounter took an extremely dark turn.

41

+++

The unmarked black van parked around the corner from an array of office buildings, hiding in plain sight among a plethora of other vehicles that didn't appear to have any reason for being there. They were not even in the only black van in the area, so no one would have suspected anything if they had cared enough to glance in their direction. The two men inside were monstrously large, mean, and dangerous. They were both of Samoan descent and they filled out every square inch of their bodies with muscle. They had only one job, and that was what they were there to do. If they got the call from their boss, then they would act and do what he paid them to do.

They watched the front door of the building on Pennsylvania Avenue in Market Square like it was going to perform a magic trick they didn't want to miss. There was only one person within that they cared anything about, and if that person exited before they got the call telling them to act one way or another, then they would have to reveal themselves and go after them. It had happened that way more times than it should have, so they hoped against hope that this time would be different. Every time the door popped open, the men got antsy. They fell back into disappointed states with each view of a face through the binoculars. The wait would need to continue.

+++

Sitting in the leather chair at the large oak desk, Logan could not help but let his jaw drop and his eyes narrow sharply. He was unable to react because of the contract he had just signed, but it was the words the man had spoken to him that really made him want to lash out violently. It wasn't like violence was a foreign concept for either of them. Logan did everything he could not to even say a word that Nestor would find untoward. He made no attempt to hide the contempt he was feeling with his facial expressions. If anyone had seen him, there would have been no mistaking that he was livid about something, though there would never

42

be a situation in which a person would come close to guessing what had him so upset.

"You have got to be fucking kidding me," thought Logan. *"There is no way that motherfucker just said what I think I heard him say. If he did, then he will be lucky to get out of this room alive...or I will."*

"Would you mind repeating that?" asked Logan, staying as clam as he could but brimming with fury. "I am not sure I heard you correctly."

"Don't fuck with me. I know full-well that you heard exactly what I said, and you will do it if you are going to join this organization," said Nestor.

"No, I may have heard you, but I am not really sure that you are serious."

"I am deadly serious. You lied to this organization when you signed that contract. You now have to pay the price for that."

"I lied? About what?" asked Logan. "I signed the contract like you asked."

"In the questionnaire it asked about family and said you needed to cut all familial ties. Do you recall reading that part?" asked Nestor.

"Of course I remember it. It happened less than five minutes ago."

"Do you see your answer?" asked Nestor, thrusting the paper into Logan's face.

"Yeah, I see it. So what?"

"It says you have no family. No ties to speak of. That's a fucking lie!"

"How is that a lie?" asked Logan. "I don't have family ties to speak of."

"You son of a bitch," said Nestor. "I was in your fucking house twice. I saw the pictures and your ring. Did you post pictures of the neighbor's kids and wife?"

"Oh, shit," Logan said under his breath.

"Yeah, so you admit it. You lied."

"I didn't want to tell you about them, no. I didn't do it to lie."

"I don't care what your bullshit reason was. You lied and per the contract you read and signed, there is no place for liars and people we cannot trust within this organization."

"I still won't do it. That request is inhuman. How the fuck can you even ask me to do something so heinous?"

"Because they are your familial ties, and the contract states you must cut ties with them. It also explicitly states that any lie will have consequences. This is the consequence of your lie. If you want this job, you have to do it."

"I refuse. If I don't take this job, it isn't the end of the fucking world for me. I have my money, I have my skills, and I can always go back to working for myself."

"Um, not so fast, Logan…uh, I mean, Vapor. There is another section you are forgetting about."

"What, pray tell, is that, Nestor?" asked Logan, confused by the man's assertion he was forgetting something important enough that it needed to be brought up at such a strange moment.

"Section 10, the last fucking page, says 'Any member or prospective member who refuses to complete a job for the organization under order of someone in authority over them, shall forfeit all rights to the organization and become target of the unit of hunters within, receiving a 24-hour start before the hunt begins.'"

"What the fuck? Are you telling me that in that contract it says that if I don't do what you just told me to do, I am officially a target of the Animal Kingdom?"

"That's exactly what I am telling you. As of this moment, your refusal to complete the task I have assigned you to guarantee your employment here, has officially made you a target. We will start hunting you in twenty-four hours. If I were you, I would find a damn good place to hide. We always get our man."

"You don't have to do this. You know who I am and what I am capable of. My advice is don't try this. It will not end well for you."

"I guess we will find out sooner rather than later. To think, all you had to do was what I asked. All you had to do was kill two people."

"All I had to do was kill two people? Is that really how you see it?"

"I don't give a fuck if they were your wife and daughter. An order is an order in this organization. Look where refusing has gotten you."

"You are a sick fuck, Nestor."

Nestor picked up the phone and dialed a few numbers. When someone picked up on the other end, he uttered one simple phrase that sent chills down Logan's spine. He had no idea what he was going to do now that he had engaged a dangerous group of hunter-killers in a game of cat-and-mouse. He glared as Nestor spoke.

"Do it now, and get her to the dungeon."

CHAPTER FIVE

Logan ran from the building so quickly that the pain in his body was almost nonexistent and his breath was short before he reached his vehicle parked a few blocks away. He was certain beyond words that Nestor was talking about his wife, so the next logical step was to protect Anisa since she would undoubtedly be next. There was no way that even Nestor was ballsy enough to take a child who wasn't his from a school surrounded by guards, police, parents, and gates. Prince Junior High and High School was the most prestigious in the area, and they went to great lengths sparing no expense to ensure that their student body was completely cared for and safe. Logan himself had issues more than once picking up his own child, and that was with a photo ID and his name on the list of approved guardians.

He drove as if he were headed for a house on fire to rescue the last living occupants, ignoring any and all street and road signs, pretending lights didn't exist, and going around cars he thought were going too slow. When he finally got to the school, there was already a row of cars there to pick up students for a variety of reasons. He would not be able to quickly get his daughter and get away as he had hoped. He only trusted that the Animal Kingdom would not come for her as quickly as he had decided to.

He waited until his turn and then went into the visitor's parking zone in front of the main door of the building and tried to calmly walk inside. He was rushing his pace at the same time he tried to convey that there was nothing amiss. He didn't know how people would read him, but at this point, he honestly didn't really care a whole lot. He finally reached the secretary's desk and told the girl there, Rachel, who he was there to retrieve. She called it out over the PA and after five minutes an extremely confused Anisa walked down the hallway with all of her books in tow.

"Hey, daddy."

"Hey, sweetie. You need to come with me. I will explain everything on the way."

"Um, okay. Where are we going?"

"I will tell you everything in the car. We don't have time to waste. Let's go." He pressed her back and hurried her along like a parent might do to a child in a store that was taking too much time going from place to place.

Anisa had no complaints about following her dad, but she was more than a little curious about why she was being pulled out of school in the middle of the day with no explanation immediately forthcoming. She walked behind her dad a little ways once he removed his hand from her back. She couldn't help but think about a million different reasons that this could be happening, but none of them made enough sense that her dad wouldn't say what it was while also being bad enough to need her to leave school. Family emergency was her first thought, but her dad would never keep something like that to himself.

Once in the car and buckled, Anisa looked at her dad who was showing signs of genuine panic. He was shaking a little, though almost imperceptibly to someone who didn't know him, and sweat was beading on his forehead. She didn't want to ask questions, but he wasn't exactly volunteering anything at the moment either. She waited for him to be ready, and despite it taking a while, he eventually found the words to say to her.

"I'm sorry, kiddo. I know you're wondering what is going on. Your mom was taken by some bad men. It has to do with some people I was working with. I am worried they will come for you next, so I need to get you to safety. For now, you will come with me to my safe house until I can figure out something more permanent."

"What do you mean mom was taken? Like, kidnapped?" asked Anisa.

"Yes, like kidnapped. They are bad men, and I don't know what they plan to do with her, but I will not let them get their hands on you if that's their goal."

"Daddy, who are you working for if they took mom because of something you did?"

"I do business with a lot of people, baby. Some are good and others are not. This group is not good."

"But, your job has put mom in danger. Why aren't you trying to get her back instead of coming to me? Do you love me more than her?"

"What? No, absolutely not. I love you both equally, but you I can take care of, she is already gone. Once I have you safe, then I will go find her and get her to safety too."

They drove for hours across main roads and hidden side roads and it wasn't long before Anisa lost complete track of where they were and just let herself drift off to sleep instead. As she slept, Logan wove through a maze of streets that a great majority of people in the world didn't know even existed. When he got to a road that was part dirt and part rock he eased onto it and traveled down it cautiously. Too much speed and he would go spinning out of control. Too little speed and the ride would be bumpy and uncomfortable. When he got to the end of that road, there was a grass field that he crossed and the car came to a paved parking spot in front of a small cabin that was only large enough for two rooms and a bathroom.

The cabin was made of strong oak and was a dark brown color that hid well in the darkness. There was only one door in the front, so no way to exit through the rear. There was one window on either side of the door, and none on the sides and back of the structure. The single light on the wood above the door came on upon their approach. As the headlights illuminated it in the fading sunlight, it looked somehow even smaller than it had before. Logan rolled his eyes at needing to be here and then stepped out. He opened the other door and roused Anisa who took a moment to orient herself to the new surroundings.

"Daddy, where are we?" asked Anisa, looking in all directions and recognizing nothing. She had never been to any place that so much as resembled this place, and it made her nervous. She wondered to herself how her dad even knew about this location, but she let it go as soon as it finished in her head.

"This is a house a friend of mine owns," lied Logan with relative ease. "I called him and told him I needed it and he said we could stay here for as long as we needed."

"It doesn't look like a regular cabin," she said observantly. "I mean, it is so small and I don't see windows or doors."

"Yeah, he likes his privacy, I guess. As far as this place goes, I hope we won't need to be here for too long. I am trying to figure out some way to get you to a safe place by tomorrow at the latest."

When they entered the interior, there was nothing inside except for a sofa and a rocking chair. There were no pictures on the walls, no television or radio. There was nothing that made it seem anything like a home. It was more of a hiding spot, and anyone with knowledge of such things who entered would have no doubt that was exactly where they had come. The only place to sleep was on the sofa, unless someone was willing to sleep on a hardwood floor with a blanket for a mattress and a bedsheet as a blanket.

There was a power outlet, so Anisa plugged in her phone and chatted with friends and played games. She didn't mention anything about where she was due to explicit orders from her dad, but she did say that she may not be back at school for a while. She didn't want people asking questions if she didn't show up the following day. They would already be curious about her absence in the back half of the current day.

After a while, both Anisa and Logan grew tired from boredom and fell asleep. They slept so well that the following day they didn't awaken early, or even before noon. It was not until Logan woke up at 1pm that he shook Anisa awake and they left to get food at a nearby diner. After eating they went back to the cabin and went about their business. Logan was reading a news article on his phone when he heard a car engine in the distance.

He ran to the window, still limping from the injury and surgery, and threw open the curtain, staring into the expanse. He could hear it before he could see it, but as he watched a black SUV made its way on the dirt-rock road. It was coming in his direction. He knew that since there was nothing else at the end of the road, and turning onto the grass was not logical, but the only option left if you got that far.

"Anisa, get up, we need to go!" shouted Logan.

Hearing her panicked father's voice she stood up with her phone in her hand and ran to him. She could see the vehicle he was staring at and she felt a kind of uneasiness as well. She understood on some level why they were here, so when she saw people that shouldn't be there approaching, she knew instinctively that something was flawed.

"Daddy, who are they?" Anisa asked.

"I don't know, but they definitely mean trouble for us. We need to get out of here, now."

Listening to her dad, she followed him as he walked out of the door and toward the car. They had almost made it when the first shot rang out. It pierced the driver's door of the vehicle. It was followed by too many more to count that painted the air around them and hit the wood of the cabin in various spots, chipping off pieces upon impact. Logan grabbed Anisa and pushed her down, covering her like a tarp. The bulk of his body faced the shooters from the SUV and he refused to let a single grain of dirt touch her.

When the shooting stopped, he stood up in front of her, still guarding her from the lurking danger, and dragged her by putting his arms behind his back and dragging her, keeping her in his grip as he went along. He made it to the car and pushed her roughly inside. He felt for the moment that she was safe enough on the floorboard and decided to make his own attempt at getting to the driver's side door. When he stepped out, the driver tried in vain to hit him with the front bumper. He struck the fender of the car instead. Logan dove back out of sight and hid behind the back tire. He realized now that they were out of bullets and he had an easier out than he originally thought.

He ran around the back bumper and to the front door, flinging it open and diving in. two men jumped out of the SUV and came toward his still-open door but he put it in reverse immediately after starting it and avoided them. He careened past the SUV when he was able to put it in gear, the jolt forcing the door closed. He sped away with Anisa still in the floor, but when they were far enough away, she slipped back into the seat and buckled herself in tightly. She was crying, and the tears were staining her face. Logan did not know how to console her, and at the moment he couldn't actually do anything since he had to get them to safety.

When he got to the center of the city, he decided to keep driving all the way to the airport. He had formulated a plan in his mind that he believed was the best option for both of them. He had to protect her, but he also had to be alone to find Janet and end the threat against his own life that he had chosen not to tell his daughter about. He knew she was frightened enough and didn't need anything else to fear or worry about. If she knew her dad was also in danger, she would not cope well with it. She was accustomed to him being gone for periods of time, but she was far from prepared to lose him forever.

He parked in the lot and the two of them got out and walked inside. There was a large crowd of people there, but most of them were not waiting in lines. It was just maneuvering the masses to get to the lines that was difficult. Logan had Anisa's hand pulled her with him as he walked. They got to a counter where a man was ready to help them and Logan purchased two tickets to California. Anisa had never even left DC so she was weirdly excited about a trip, but didn't want to show too much emotion in that regard given their circumstances.

They went to their gate and waited for the flight to board. They were on Delta flight 1631, a nonstop from Dulles to Los Angeles. They would arrive roughly six hours from the time they took off and it would put them in town at about 6pm local time. They would have dinner and then Logan would take her where she would be safest. He could think of nowhere on earth that she would be any safer. He would never let anything happen to her, Logan was sure in a way he had never been about anything else.

Dinner was good and necessary, and Anisa had tried foods she had
never had an opportunity to try before like real Mexican cuisine and
desserts that she didn't know existed. After they finished, they took their
rented car and Logan drove for two long hours. He had grown up in
California for a lot of his life, but he was going to a place he had only just
learned about when he looked for the man he was coming to see. He had
no idea Logan was coming, and he might or might not be pleased to see
him. When Logan got to a place called Holbrook Desert, he knew he had
found what he was looking for.

It was small for a city, if it could even be called that, and finding the
man was going to be hard even for a place so miniscule. If nothing else,
the man could hide like it was his job. At times, it had been his job and
he had taught Logan to become great at it as well, making his future
career choices much smoother.

He had a street name from a deep search on the internet, but an address
was not something he would put in such an accessible location. The only
reason the street name was there was because he had to register it when
he was stopped with a firearm on a traffic checkpoint. He had refused to
give details, Logan was sure, so the court was probably willing to bend
and accept the street name so they could at the least track him to a locale.

Finding the street, Logan knew why it was just a street. There was not
another house of any kind visible for as far as the eye could see. There
was only a small dilapidated shack of a house at the end of the road. It
was hidden behind some trees and bushes, but Logan's eyes were trained
enough that he could see it was there. He had some preconceived notions
about what to expect, but clearly the man had changed with age.

He turned onto the road and slowly made his way to the driveway that
touched the paved part of the roadway. He turned left onto it and pulled
as close to the house as he could. He heard a shotgun blast that he knew
to be directed at the air and didn't even flinch. The same could not be
said for Anisa who screamed like she had been hit by the shell. Logan

patted her leg to let her know it was okay and she was safe. He stayed in the car and waited for the old man to come to him, which didn't take too long.

"Who the fuck are you?" demanded the man. "Why the fuck are you on my property? Get the fuck out of here before I blow a fucking whole through you with this shotgun!"

"Able, it's me, Logan," he said, still not quite ready to get out and risk a shotgun blast.

"Logan?"

"Yeah, dad, it's me."

"The hell are you doing here? How the fuck did you find me?"

Logan laughed loud enough for Able to hear him and he didn't look pleased. "You taught me everything I know, you old bastard."

"True. Now answer the other one. Why are you here?"

"I need your help, and I need it now."

"You can't just show up after this long and expect me to offer my help to you. I mean, you basically forgot all about me when you left here."

"You told me to. You said forget you so no one could put us together. They never did. I wouldn't be here if it wasn't absolutely essential. You are the last place I would ever go, and now you are the last option."

"Well, better go ahead and tell me what it is you need so I can tell you to fuck off and send you on your merry way."

"It's not really for me. It's for her," Logan said, pointing at the girl seated in the front seat that he had somehow until that moment failed to notice.

"Who is this?" asked Able.

"My daughter," said Logan flatly.

"Oh? And how did that happen? I heard some shit about you that has me a little worried the training went in one ear and out the other."

"I met a woman a lot of years ago, fell in love, married her, and then we had Anisa. Pretty straightforward."

"Really? I never expected you to get married much less have a damn child. So, tell me what in the fuck possessed you to work for the government! I hear you went to work for the CIA and the Marine Corps." Logan looked at him with an expression of contempt. "Don't look at me that way. I damn sure raised you better than to work for the people we were trying to stop."

"I had to make a living somehow. I took jobs I knew I could complete. Sometimes they felt right and sometimes they didn't, but I always finished what I started."

"Since when do you have a conscience when it comes to pulling a fucking trigger?"

"Since I grew into the man I was always going to be. I cannot kill indiscriminately and feel okay about it. After you had me taking lives at your whim, I decided to pick and choose more carefully."

"So, you did that by working with the people we so desperately wanted no part of?" asked Able.

"No, I did that working for the people who paid me to do it."

"You sold out, you little shit. I knew you would eventually, but I thought you would have to be about my age before it came to that."

"Just how the hell do you know so much about what I have been up to, anyway, old man?"

"You may have forgot me but I didn't forget you. I kept tabs. I looked into you from time to time. I did some of the deep searches I taught you to do and found everything I wanted to know and it all pissed me right off."

"You spied on me?" asked Logan, finally climbing out of the car. "You didn't think I would go down the path you chose for me or what?"

"I needed to know what my one and only kid was up to. I wanted to be sure you knew what you were doing, and surprise, surprise, you had no fucking clue."

"Fuck you, Able," said Logan and was then met with an open-palm slap to the face that stunned him severely.

"Who do you think you are talking to? Didn't you come here for my help?"

"I do need your help…or rather she does," he said, rubbing the spot where the slap had made its impact. He could feel it reddening and getting hot. It would welt before long, but he couldn't let Able know that it felt painful. What he really wanted was to dish one out on the man in retaliation, but that would have all but guaranteed he didn't help them, and they needed him now.

"What do you want? I don't have the time to listen to bullshit, so make it fast."

He first introduced Anisa to the man, though she was terrified of him after watching him slap her father, the bravest and strongest man she had ever known. "My wife, Janet, her mother, was kidnapped by a dangerous man from a dangerous organization, and they will be coming for her next. I need somewhere she can be safe while I do what it is that I do and get Janet back."

"You want her to stay here with me while you go on a mission to get mommy back? Do I have that correct?"

"Basically, yes. I really have nowhere else to turn. If there was anyone else, I would be there instead of here."

"How long are you needing me to watch her? I can keep her here for as long as you need, but I am gonna need some money to make sure she has everything she needs while she is here."

"You cheap fuck! Fine, I will give you some money, and I will come check on her as soon as I can. It might be several days, weeks, god only knows. I just need to know she is safe all the time."

"I have an arsenal inside the house, I can take care of us both. You have nothing to worry about."

"Good. She can use a weapon too, so don't hesitate to let her help out if it comes to that. I have been training her since she was ten."

"So, you thought enough of what I taught you to teach it to your own child. I'm honored."

"I thought it was important for her to know how to protect herself. Don't read too much into it."

"Whatever you say," Able said with clear doubt about Logan's intentions in teaching his daughter the same skills he had taught Logan all those years before.

Logan wrote a number on a small piece of paper using the pen he had taken from the meeting with Nestor and handed both the pen and paper to his daughter. She took it with some hesitation, and Logan did everything in his power to prevent rolling his eyes when he saw that stupid fake tattoo that Anisa wore on her index finger. It was a blight on her otherwise smooth skin, and it irritated Logan to no end that she wore it believing that it somehow added value or character. He brought his focus back to where it belonged.

Able and Logan talked about the specifics of the tenure Anisa would have with Able and then she hugged her dad tightly for several minutes before he walked away from her. He knew she was safe, at least for now, and he planned to come back for her, or at least to check on her, within a week. He hated once again leaving her behind for an unknown amount of time, but he knew beyond a doubt that this was by far the most necessary instance of doing so.

+++

It didn't take long for Anisa to get comfortable with Able and her new living situation. She wasn't going to have to attend school, traditionally anyway, since Able was going to homeschool her until Logan came back. She could eat what she wanted and when, had no bed time, and could call Logan any time she needed using the number he had given her on the little piece of paper. Able couldn't get fully used to the idea that he was more or less a grandfather, though Logan was not his birth child. He fell quickly for Anisa and her winning personality. They bonded and soon began to enjoy one another's company.

"Able," said Anisa. "What were you and my dad talking about when we pulled up?"

"What do you mean?" he asked, not sure where she was going with the question.

"You and him were talking about him killing people. What did you mean?"

"Oh that? It's not literal sweetheart. He didn't really kill anyone. Can you imagine if he did? That would make him as bad as the people he is chasing to get your mom back."

"So, why did you say it that way? Why did you and him both say 'kill' so much like it wasn't a code?"

"Well, it is a way for him not to say what he really does for a living. A kill just refers to people that he worked with or did some kind of business with."

"Still seems weird to me," she said seriously.

"Your dad is kind of a strange person. He always was. From the moment I took him in, he was a bit of an odd guy. I guess he never grew out of it. Must have gotten it from his real dad."

"Real dad? What are you talking about?" asked Anisa.

Not realizing she didn't know the truth, he figured out fast that he had put his foot in his mouth. He decided it wasn't his place but he had already opened the door, so he told her the truth about how the two had come into one another's lives. As he spoke, she listened intently to every word he said. She was sad and grateful. Without Able, who knew what may have become of her father. The law would have had him in foster care and perhaps never finding a forever family like so many other kids in the same kind of system. He did keep out the parts about teaching him to fire a rifle and taking him on missions to kill people and take their money or belongings. She was enthralled by the story and had so many questions. Able answered all of them, and before they knew it, the time had crept away and it was after midnight. They both went to bed and slept peacefully, waiting for the next day, their first full day together.

+++

Logan made a bold and risky move to go to his house when he got back to DC and collect weapons in preparation for the brewing conflict between himself and the Animal Kingdom. He was putting handguns in a bag when his phone rang. He looked at the caller ID and saw that it was a local call and ignored it. The caller tried again and was ignored again. He tossed the phone on the sofa and accidentally hit the button to answer it. He didn't realize what he had done, but the caller was using the active phone to track its location.

Logan felt comfortable at home, but he knew he couldn't stay there long. It was bound to be one of the first places that they came to look for him, though it was unlikely they would think him dumb enough to go to the one place that would mark him as an easy target. He was sitting on the recliner in the living room, watching television, when the front door was kicked off of its hinges and a group of three armed men stormed in with weapons drawn.

Logan ducked out of the way, falling over the arm of the chair to do so. He retrieved the pistol from his waistband and rolled into a better position for aiming and shooting. He fired once and missed his target, and he was met with a barrage of gunfire from an automatic rifle. It ripped the cotton and wood of the chair to shreds and Logan moved quickly to a better spot near the sofa. They could not see him there and he took the opportunity to fire again, this time hitting his target with ease. He did so again, and the next target went down. The third man having seen and heard where the shots came from discharged his weapon, emptying the magazine in to the sofa and wall behind it. He didn't hit Logan, but he had chased him out of hiding.

Logan dropped his weapon when he jumped up from his perch and was met with the bottom of a foot to his chest as he charged. He fell backward, and then pushed himself to his feet with some effort. With his hands still on the floor pushing, the blow to his ribcage was felt with all the force behind it. He fell over once again. When the man came toward him, he rolled, grabbed the left leg and yanked him to the floor, rolling again, this time toward the body, and dropping two sequential elbows to the chest, knocking the wind out of the man. He got to his feet gingerly and then stepped on the man's throat. He was gasping for air, but Logan didn't let up for a second. He had moved enough to reach the dropped pistol with a stretch, and he reached over and picked it up. He took up aim at the man's forehead and held it there.

"You and your boss have fucked with the wrong man! You are my message to him! Sorry it has to be this way," he said, and fired the weapon, slicing a hole through the skull and emitting a jet of blood flow. The pool that formed behind the head was similar to spilled oil on the hardwood. It spread and then stopped when as much came out as could have before it congealed. Logan dropped the weapon and left the house with all of the others he had packed for this sort of occasion.

Logan knew he was in real trouble. He didn't learn enough about the Animal Kingdom in his short time interacting with its leader, but clearly there was more to them than he had assumed at the start. He had already had violent encounters with a dozen of them, and it seemed there would be more to come. If he had not yet seen the men who were named after hunters, then he had not yet made it to the crux of the organization. There was no telling how many more he would have to go through before meeting those he would have been working hand-in-hand with. That knowledge gave him a new perspective and he knew right away that was going to have to take drastic measures if he was going to survive. He thought about a specific dead man, one he had killed, the one who started him on his journey. The dead mad held answers he didn't know he had, but the question remained: after what he had done, would they be willing to help him?

CHAPTER SIX

The two large Samoan men dragged Janet into the dungeon room at a separate building from the one where Logan had met with Nestor. It was a solid concrete room with nothing on the ceiling, walls, or floor. The only thing in the room was the door through which the three of them had entered. There was little lighting inside so there were shadows bouncing around. One of the men held on to her while another left briefly and then returned carrying a steel chair that he placed in the center of the room and screwed to the floor. Janet was then thrown unceremoniously onto it and strapped down with cords and ties. There was nothing beyond simple flicks of her wrists and ankles that she could do. Her head was left alone, but she had a terrified look in her blue eyes.

The room was cold and Janet was wearing only a short sleeve dress which did nothing to abate the temperature. She shivered with no way to stop what she was feeling. Neither man left the room now. They both stood in front of her and watched her like they were predators and her the ultimate prey. They had been given clear instructions not to harm her or let her come to any kind of harm. Nestor had special plans for her and allowing her to be harmed beforehand would take away a lot of the thrill.

After several hours, Janet was left alone in the pitch black of the room. She had been fed and given water, something she received every hour on the hour, and she still couldn't move and found it hard to breathe at times. She was afraid and worried, but she had hope that Logan would find her and free her. The only thing she didn't know was when it would happen. She knew exactly what her husband did for a living now. She had secretly read his messages over and over. Some of them with details that made her stomach turn. He was more than capable of rescuing her, as long as he still loved her enough to try and do so. It was no secret to him that she didn't love him or their daughter. She just prayed that his feelings were strong enough that he would come and get her. It was possible he cared so little that he didn't even yet know that she had been taken.

She fell asleep late in the evening and awakened still tied to the steel chair. Her back was hurting and she had a headache, but she was still alive, which was all she could ask for at the moment. She assumed someone would tell her why she had been taken, but if they refused to do that, then she would assume instead that it was from something her husband had either said or done. She was still coming to when the door opened and a huge man, taller than her husband, stood like a statue in the doorway, staring at her. The light was just enough that she could see his sneer. He walked slowly toward her, each step closer making her feel less at ease.

"Janet Aster. My name is Nestor Jacobson. You are here because your husband didn't care enough about you to do a simple job that I asked him to complete."

"What do you mean? What kind of job?" asked Janet, fear settling in.

"Oh, that's between him and us. Suffice it to say, he is going to be suffering the consequences of his actions."

"How long am I here for? Do I have to stay in this damn chair?"

"You will stay here with us until your husband pays his debts. As soon as that is done, we will let you go like none of this ever happened."

"I want to sleep in a bed and get out of this chair."

"I don't trust you enough for that. You are the wife of one of the most dangerous men I have ever met. I doubt that he didn't teach you a thing or two about how to survive."

Janet's mind immediately went to the past. It was weeks after they were married and things were still amazing between them. They were in love and looking toward the future that held so much promise. In the first few lessons, Logan had taught her defensive stances. It had taken some time to learn all of them, but she eventually got it down almost as well as he had them. Once they got past that, he jumped into defensive moves. This was even harder, but Janet had pulled through and knew everything she was supposed to. After that, they segued into a hand-to-hand combat training that taught her how to fight in close quarters. He had then moved to various weapons to train her with, and she could now fire any weapon, use any blade, and basically make a weapon from anything she could get her hands on. Yes, he had definitely taught her a thing or two. If she got free of her bindings, she would lay it on them thick.

'I have no idea what the hell you are talking about," she lied easily. "My husband is a financial worker who helps wealthy people with investments and the like."

"Yes, I am sure that's what he told you. He's a liar. He is a hired killer and has been for a very long time."

"You're lying," she said in mock horror. Her face was red and there were tears in her eyes. They were real, but they were not from the conversation like she wanted Jacobson to believe they were. She was genuinely scared and unsure of what was coming for her.

"I apologize ahead of time," he said insincerely. "There is going to be a bit more to this than you sitting in a chair, waiting for your useless husband to pay what he owes."

Janet gulped, understanding at that second that the man intended to wound her, to make her regret being married to the man who had led them to such a point. He was unlikely to let her walk away unscathed, but she wondered to herself whether that meant alive too. The thought had just finished when he whacked her in the temple with the butt of a pistol and everything went immediately dark.

+++

Logan was on his way to the airport yet again. He was headed for Mexico to meet a man who had no love for him whatsoever. It all began with the first kill he had ever made. He was told he was killing a man who stole from a rich mogul. When he had seen on the financial records that the man was giving a lot of money to a criminal organization, it never dawned on him that the organization would be angry that they were losing so much money. When someone had told the leader of the organization that it was him who was responsible, there had been a hit ordered that Logan had avoided for over twenty years. He was on the verge of walking into the den of the man who had ordered the hit and still wanted him to pay for what he had done. Before booking the trip, he had asked a contact if it was still active and he was told with emphasis that it most certainly was. He welcomed the risk he was taking because the payoff could be more than worth it in the end.

When he got on the plane, he was seated in the middle where he usually liked to be. There were a lot of empty seats, and he felt at ease knowing there would be no screaming kids, angry fat people, or seat-mates to smash him into the window of the plane. He quickly fell asleep before the plane had even taken off from the ground. He felt the wheels lift from the pavement and pull him from true sleep, but he ignored it in his tired state, drifting right off again.

The turbulence was bad but he was able to sleep through it for the most part. It jostled him awake a few times. He was always able to fall back into his slumber. It was when he heard the woman scream that he jumped from his seat. It was followed by more screams and he knew something was wrong. He moved toward the sounds and saw a man holding a gun with a silencer. He didn't recognize the man, but he knew there was nothing he could offer but trouble. He pressed further forward.

When the man saw him, he fired a silenced round that hit the seat close to him. The only time turbulence was asked for was when it could stop a madman from shooting you at 35,000 feet in the air. That bump had been timed perfectly. Logan dove behind a seat and waited until the man either moved or made a mistake.

"Logan Aster!" the man yelled. "This is on you. Come out now or there will be others." He grabbed a woman from a nearby seat and shot her in the side of her head and dropped her body like a stone. Logan gasped. This man was here for him and he was going to kill innocent people unless he gave himself up. He was torn between risking his life to save the others and letting them die so he could get a better read on the killer. He had no qualms letting people die who he thought deserved it, but this was something else entirely.

Logan stepped out and put his hands in the air. From behind the man, which he had seen, the air marshal charged and tackled the shooter. This gave Logan time enough to clamber out of his hiding spot and attack. The killer rolled around with the marshal for a few seconds before getting off a shot into his chest that rendered him dead on impact. Logan jumped on the shooter and punched him in the face, blood spraying from his parted lips. He threw another two punches, one with each fist and both connecting. The man took them easily and then struck Logan with a kick to his midsection, doubling him over for a brief second. He got to his feet and delivered an uppercut to his chin that sent him reeling backward.

Jumping on Logan in his vulnerable state, he placed the gun to his chest and tried to pull the trigger, but Logan had placed his thumb in the way. At the same time, he yanked the weapon away and threw it down the aisle. No one dared to pick it up so it sat on the floor and slid around with the jumpiness of the plane. Logan grabbed the man by the shirt collar and pulled him close to his face. He head-butted him directly in the forehead and sent him sprawling. He hit the back of his head on the bottom of one of the seats. As soon as he landed, all of the passengers fled for other parts of the cabin.

The man wobbled to his feet and tried to lunge for Logan, but he was caught and put into a headlock that prevented him from using his arms. Logan took the opportunity to sweep his feet and drop him to his knees. He was detained and Logan didn't know what to do with him. It was still a long way to Mexico so there was no way he could hold him for the remainder of the flight. He balled his fist and clocked him on the side of the head and left him unconscious.

He ran for the cockpit to tell the flight crew what was going on, wondering the whole time why no one had already done it. He told a short, fat man in an aisle seat to watch the man, and if he moved, he was supposed to yell for Logan. The man grudgingly agreed, though Logan had his serious doubts about whether or not the passenger would do as he was asked. He looked mortified to have been put in such a position as it was.

Knocking on the cockpit door, Logan was not sure that anyone would answer. When a woman in a pilot's uniform did pull the door open, she did so with a gun in his face. She looked scared and angry. He green eyes were narrowed and her red hair was ruffled as though she had been running her hands through it. "What do you want?" she asked.

"I am a passenger on the plane. I have subdued an unruly passenger who killed two people. We need to land this fucking plane now."

"We are already working on it, sir," she said condescendingly. "Now, please go away."

Logan was pissed off but he complied. He was halfway back when the fat man screamed. "Sir, he's up!" Logan ran as fast as he could, his back pain flaring up as he did so, and he just missed the man as he opened the door to the diving plane and leapt out with a parachute on his back.

"Where the fuck did that come from?" wondered Logan as he watched the man falling. He didn't want to do what came next, but he was out of options. The man had tried to kill him and had taken the lives of two other people on the plane. He couldn't be allowed to live. He grabbed the gun, ran to the door, gauged how far the man had fallen, and then dove like he was springing from the diving board into a massive pool. He fell freely through the sky, his stomach somewhere up in his throat. He did what he knew to do to increase speed and placed his hands by his sides and speared toward the man. If he missed, he would be dead. If he caught him, he might still die, but he would go down fighting. He still didn't know who the man was, who he worked for, how he knew who he was, or why he wanted him dead. It was too bad those questions would have to remain unanswered forever.

He was gaining on the man and he looked back just in time to spot him and stare in horror. He couldn't go any quicker and if Logan reached him, he knew without a doubt that he would kill him. Logan almost smiled as he was within striking distance. He reached out and grabbed the foot and pulled, forcing his own body forward. Before too long, he was face to face with the man and there was nothing either of them could do. Logan tried to punch and the man retaliated but they both missed badly. Logan didn't want to do it 30,000 feet in the air, but he took out the pistol and pointed at the man's head. He peed himself in utter terror. Without so much as a hesitation, Logan fired three times into the head of the flying target. His head jolted back with each one though he was dead after the first.

Still falling shockingly fast, Logan ripped the parachute off of the man and then snapped it around his own chest. He still had a long way to go before the chute needed to be opened, but now he had the peace of mind that when he was that low, he would be able to land safely. He had no idea where the killer's body had fallen. Someone was in for a real surprise in a few minutes. He fell to the appropriate height of just over 4,000 feet and ripped the cord. Nothing happened, and the chute did not deploy as it should have. He continued to fall, but more panicky than before. He reached for the cord to the reserve chute with trembling fingers. He slipped off of it three times and then finally was able to get a secure grip. He yanked it and then the chute extended from the pack the way it should have, but he was dangerously close to the rocky ground when it finally did. He was still falling at high speeds when he hit the earth hard enough to rattle him, but not so hard that it caused any damage. He had no idea where he was or how close he was to his ultimate destination. He threw off the bag and walked to find answers in the nearest town.

The sign near the road almost a mile away told him that there was a town only five miles behind him. While it was hot and that was kind of a long way to walk in the current conditions, he had no choice. He didn't even know if he was still in America since he was heading out of the country to begin with. As he walked the hot route, he realized he had not eaten or had anything to drink since boarding the plane. If he did not get where he was going soon, he was going to be dead and all of his effort would be wasted anyway.

After two hours of walking, he made it a small convenience store where he bought water and asked the clerk about where he was. He drank the bottle in the store without taking a second sip and then rested his hands on the counter and stared into the eyes of the suddenly frightened young teenager behind it. "Where the hell am I?" he asked.

"Wh-wh-wh-what do you mean?" asked the kid who wore a nametag that said Jared. He was not tall or short and had earrings in both of his ears. He was smiling until Logan approached him and made him feel intimidated.

"I mean I don't know where here is and I need to know."

"Like the city, or the state?" asked Jared.

"Yes, I need to know what city and state I am in."

"Oh, you are in Blalock, Arizona," the boy said, his demeanor becoming more inviting and less afraid. "If you are here, why don't you know where you are?"

"My plane had engine trouble and I had to parachute out," he said to the boy who looked genuinely impressed.

"Oh, I see. You are lucky to be alive then, I guess."

"You could certainly say that," said Logan. "How far am I from Mexico?"

"Oh, you are not far at all. Maybe a few hours if you catch a bus. There is a station right down the road. You can pay in cash. Do you want me to tell you how to get there?"

"Yeah, I would appreciate that," said Logan. "Thanks for your help." He dropped a wad of money onto the countertop as a thank you after the boy told him what he needed to know and then headed for the bus that would get him where he most desperately needed to go.

The bus took him south to Mexico, past the border, and into the heart of Mexico City where he departed and rented a car. He drove to the compound that was hidden from the public and that only the most unsavory of people knew anything about. As he drove down dirt roads and back alleys, all he could think about was the unexpected greeting he was in for. There was no guarantee of any kind that they would not shoot and kill him on sight. He was hoping they would at least let him make his offer before they took such measures.

There in the distance it stood against the brown of the canyon walls. It looked like just another part of the landscape until he was close enough. He could see the guards all around the exterior and the entrance that was going to be harder to breach without permission than Fort Knox. He stopped the car about the length of three football fields away and walked the rest of it. It was slow going, but he finally made it to the metal gate that surrounded the entirety of the compound.

The guard there did not hesitate for a second before training a rifle on his chest and motioning him away with his angry gestures. Ignoring them, Logan moved closer. The man motioned him away again, this time with a gruffer forceful movement of the weapon.

"I'm not fucking leaving," said Logan simply. "I am here to see Torrance."

"No one sees Torrance unless he wants to see them. He hasn't asked for you, so get the fuck out of here before I blow a hole through your chest."

"I am sure he will want to see me. He has wanted me dead for about twenty years."

"You think you are the only person to try that bullshit?" asked the guard who was dark skinned and muscle-bound.

"No, but I am positive I am the only one for whom it is true."

"I will ask him, but if he says no, you are a dead man anyway."

"Good for you then that I came prepared to die. Call him and tell him Logan Aster is at the gate."

At the mention of the name the guard looked excited as if the name was something they were taught about and should enjoy hearing. It was like the end of that man's life would bring happiness to everyone. He almost smiled except for the attempt remain professional. He picked up the phone and spoke into it briefly. He didn't change his expression a single bit while talking and then he hung up. "Torrance says don't move. He will be out in a moment."

"I'm not going anywhere," said Logan.

A jeep drove to the gate and out hopped an older man who had gray hair and an obviously dyed full beard. He was dark skinned as well and his eyes were almost gray like his hair. He was strong looking for his age, 61, and he moved with a quickness that surprised Logan.

"Mr. Torrance?" asked Logan.

"Yes," he said flatly. "You are lucky to be alive, Mr. Aster. There are a lot of people here who want you dead, including me."

"I know that. I was hoping you would let me talk before you decided to put a bullet in my brain, though."

"It wasn't going to be quite so quick or painless, but I see your point. The only reason I didn't have my guard apprehend you was that I figure there must be a reason you traveled here from America and stepped foot on my land knowing there was still an active kill order out for you."

"There is a reason. I need help."

Looking genuinely stunned, Torrance took a step backward. He laughed briefly but caught himself. "I gotta say, that was not what I was expecting to hear. In fact, of all the things I was thinking about, that didn't come up as one."

"I know, it is an unusual request, but I would love to explain it to you."

"Mr. Aster, why in the hell would I want to help you at all? You are wanted by this cartel for one simple reason: you killed our top financier and put us in dire straits for years. You have nothing to offer me."

"Never say never," he said. "I would love to talk to you about it indoors. It is hot as hell out here, and I have been through a bit much today. Someone tried to…you know what, I will tell you if you agree to house me. I will even do it with the caveat that if you don't like what I have to say, I will give myself up and you can do whatever you want. Finish the hit."

"Alright, fine. That sounds like a deal any smart businessman would not pass up. Come on in." The gate opened and he walked in and was immediately grabbed by two armed men he had not even seen until that moment in time. "They are only here to ensure you don't try anything." One of the men searched him and found no weapons since he had dropped the gun after using it on the plane killer midair.

"Oh, I have no intentions of trying anything. You don't understand how badly I need your help."

They walked together into a large conference room with a weak wooden table and some folding chairs that could be found at any Baptist church in America. They were the hard metal kind that no one liked sitting on, but when they were the only thing offered, people pretended to be comfortable with. There were no windows in the room at all and an ancient slide projector sat at the front in view of a screen that looked like it had been eaten at by a swarm of moths. Logan could not reconcile the wealth of this cartel with the state of the compound into which he had been brought. Torrance took one chair and Logan another and then everyone else left the premises.

"This is a nice place," said Logan sarcastically.

"This is an older planning room. It came about, ironically, because of what you did. When we got back on our feet, we revamped another room and now fortune 500 companies would be jealous of it."

"I am glad you found your way back to your feet, then."

"Enough chitchat. Why are you here, risking your life in Mexico when you have been outwitting us for over twenty years?"
"I need your help."

"You already said that, so I am going to give you five minutes to tell me what you need help with and why I am the one you need it from or I am going to blow your head off and busy you in the dirt of this place."

"Well, I was offered a job with a unit who wanted my skills. They said they needed someone with them since it was all they were lacking."

"I assume," said Torrance coldly, "they meant your ability to kill from a distance?"

"Yes, that. I told them yes, and they offered me a contract that I signed. Their first order was for me to kill my wife and child."

"You have a wife? You are a hitman, so how the fuck did that happen?"

"Long story. Anyway, I refused and then became a target of the unit. Since then, I have been running from them and trying to stay ahead. They kidnapped my wife Janet and I took my daughter to a safe place."

"You are a target of a unit of killers? You really fucked up, didn't you?" asked Torrance with a laugh. "I am still not hearing my part in all of this."

"The unit is big, dangerous, and prepared. I cannot get my wife back on my own, and if I fight them, I will die. I have enough skills to go after them, but not defeat them on my own. I want Diamond to work with me to stop them and help me get Janet back."

"So, you are offering us a job?"

"I guess you can look at it that way, yes."

"We don't work for free, Mr. Aster. You will have to pay our fee, and then after we finish, you are still our target as well."

"I want that wiped clean. I want to be off the hit list."

"Why would I remove you from the list? You killed the most important financier we had and put us in a hole financially for a long time. It was only when someone took up the slack that we were able to operate normally again."

"I understand that, but I did what I was asked to do. I was a child and had no idea who I was killing. Dad just told me that it would make me and him wealthy, so I went with it."

"It's that kind of shit that led you to kill without caring who people were, I guess?"

"No, it was that incident that led me to question why people needed to die. I wondered more than a few times if the person I was ordered to kill actually deserved to die."

"A hitman with a heart is always a mistake. It seems like you grew one. Married, had a child, and now care more about them than you do getting away with your own life. If I tell you no, then you're fucked."

"I know I am, but I have a proposition for you."

"Oh, do tell," the man said with a sneer. "I am sure this will be the highlight of my day."

"I will pay your fee. I will add on top of it whatever it takes to clear my name from the list. You just have to agree to help me and then let me go."

"Hmm, I don't even have a number in mind for that. I have wanted you dead so badly for so long that all I cared about was when and how that would happen. I cannot agree to that on my own. I may be a leader, but I am still required to answer to the people I work with."

"Do what you have to do, but that is my offer."

"I will agree in principle, but I need to discuss it with my men. Remember, they also want you dead and they may not be quite as reasonable a person as I am." He rose from the table and left the room, Logan sitting and staring at the seat he used to occupy.

Outside the door, Logan could hear raised, angry voices. The people were not happy and they definitely wouldn't agree without a fight. Some of them would most likely ask to change the deal to include letting him go but still hunting him, and others would never agree to let him go at all. Even though Torrance answered to others, that didn't mean he was incapable of making the decision on his own. The door flung open and a dozen men entered before Torrance at their tail.

They all stood against the wall all around the room while Torrance took his seat once again. He had a slight smile and Logan took that to mean somewhat good news. He waited for the man to speak which took several seconds after he sat back down in his seat. "The men are not agreeable to working with you. I tried to convince them, but they are unable to get over the fact that you nearly ended what we were all those years ago. The ones in this room," he pointed to the men along the walls, "were here at that time. They lived through the troublesome times and they can't forgive your crime."

"I am not asking for forgiveness," Logan said to Torrance and the room at large. "I am looking for help. I will pay you whatever you want to help me and clear my name."

"They have one small request, you know, so they are sure they can trust you."

"Okay, anything. What is it?" asked Logan.

"They want you to run for us. Drugs, guns, women. You will effectively work for us while paying us. If you cannot agree to that, then this deal is dead and so are you."

"I agree. I will do whatever you want me to do, but it comes with the condition that you help me get Janet back and save my daughter. My life is not the priority here."

"Good," said one of the men from along the wall. Torrance heard this, turned to see who it was, and then shot him in the middle of his forehead, splattering his brains on the wall behind him and dropping him to the ground dead.

"These men will show you the respect you deserve or they will meet their ends. If you work for us, you are one of us, and they will behave as such. If there is anything else, now is the time to say it. Otherwise, you will be taken to your temporary room and given your first orders."

+++

Janet was lying down on the table in the dungeon with a blindfold over her face and her appendages tied down with thick, rough cords. They were cutting into her flesh but with the surfeit of other pain she was feeling, she barely noticed. She knew she was waiting for the man with the tools because it was always the same before he arrived: tie her down and blindfold her. She was mentally preparing when she heard the door swing open.

The man came near to her and struck her right shoulder with a hammer. She screamed into the void. It was the worst pain yet, and she suddenly forgot about all of the other pain. She was crying and tears were rolling down her cheeks beneath the cover. They fell to the sides of her face and then onto the metal surface of the table.

"Where is she, you dumb bitch?" a voice said from the other side of the room. "I don't enjoy this as much as you think I do."

"I don't know," she cried through the pain. "I really don't. There is nowhere she would go. She doesn't know anyone."

"We know she was picked up from school, and after that, nothing. Where would Logan take her?" asked the voice again.

"I don't have any idea. Maybe she went with a friend from school."

"You know that's bullshit, don't you?"

"I don't know anything. We don't talk. I hate her!"

Both she and the men in the room were shocked to hear the words come out of her mouth. It was like she had eaten sand at the beach, an awful taste and feeling in her mouth. She wanted to take them back, but now it was out in the open and she knew how true it was because of the circumstances under which she had said the words. She hated her daughter and didn't care what happened to her.

"You hate her? Isn't that a bit harsh, Janet?" asked the voice.

"I do hate her. If I knew where she was, you could have her. I don't care what you do to her. She is insolent and rude. She is a daddy's girl and never gave me respect."

"You gave birth to her, didn't you? How can you hate someone you gave life?"

"She is a terrible child. She ruined my life. It would be better if she wasn't in it."

"Wow, I didn't expect that. Okay, we can try this again later. It seems like you are trying too hard to come up with reasons you won't help us, so we are going to have to think of something much worse."

The door opened once again, and Janet thought the men were leaving. When she heard a third set of feet treading on the floor, she knew someone else had made an appearance. "Boss, we have word on our guy from the plane. He tracked Aster all the way, got on the plane, attacked as planned, and was subdued. According to the flight crew, he leapt out of the plane, and Logan did the same. There is no word on either men since the incident."

"What? He jumped out of the plane? What the hell was he hoping to accomplish by doing that?"

"I don't know, boss, but the last thing we know is that both men exited through the door at 30,000 feet. It is possible both or neither are even still alive."

"Jesus, Shark. And what of the GPS device? He had it on him when he left here. Any hits on that yet?"

"Yes, boss. It activated in a small city in California. Our best guess is that he left the girl there with the device and went off on his own."

"Then we leave him alone for now. We go to California and get the girl. If he cares about her half as much as I think he does, then he will come running if he thinks she is in any danger."

"Should I send men, then?"

"Not just men, Shark. You and the hunters go yourselves. This cannot afford to be fucked up. I want progress reports every hour until that child is in your custody."

"You got it, boss." The man took out a radio and called his fellow hunters: Wolf, Jaguar, Grizzly, and Piranha. They all replied that they would meet him at the exit in the back of the building momentarily.

+++

The plan was to go back to DC eventually with the goal of taking one of the Animal Kingdom operatives for leverage, but there was the first part of the plan that had a pit stop in Texas. In Dallas, Logan was supposed to deliver a shipment of cocaine to a dealer there who was renowned for selling it both locally and across the country. It was a medium sized shipment but if they were caught, it would still mean federal prison time. Logan was unsure how to feel about what he was doing since it was so different from what he normally did, but he liked that it was getting him the help he so badly needed from the cartel.

When the drugs were successfully delivered, they drove to the next stop, a train station in Dallas, and hopped on a train headed for Washington, DC. The trip would be long but worth it. The three men, Logan, Red, and Blue, sat in a car by themselves as arranged by Torrance and figured out the plan in all its intricacies. They needed to know when to strike, how to do it, and who would be easiest to take without needing to put up too much of a fight. Logan would have loved to take a hunter, but that was not feasible. They were all dangerous in their own ways and could easily defeat anyone who attempted to put up a fight against them. They were going to have to settle for a lower-level operative, but one with enough clout that Nestor would not be able to go without exchanging him for Janet.

When they got to DC, the plan was all worked out, but they had to wait for the ideal time, so they went to the location to scout it out carefully. They knew from the intel Logan had given them that a man called Spivey would leave the building at around 9:00 in the later evening and make his way for the headquarters. As they watched the doors of the small casino, they didn't see anyone exit for a long time. It was only just past nine when it opened and their target came out a little tipsy and unsure of his steps. It was going to be easier than first thought to get the man.

Red grabbed him by the arm and turned him face-to-face. He smiled a wry, ugly smile. Crooked teeth caked with plaque from years of smoking stared Spivey right in his eyes. "Mr. Spivey, I have been sent to pick you up and get you back," he said.

"Uh," said Spivey, a short man made of muscles. "I usually drive myself, but sure. I am feeling a little bit woozy." He followed the unknown man to his own car and then got in the passenger seat. The man he didn't know climbed in the driver's seat. The two back doors opened and two more men got in, but Spivey ignored them like they didn't exist at all.

Spivey promptly fell asleep and the car drove in the other direction, away from his intended destination. When they arrived at the small house on a side street, they clambered out and Blue carried the man into the entryway and tossed him inelegantly on the sofa. The other men came in behind them and the door was slammed. When Spivey came to his senses, he was tied up to a wooden kitchen chair and his mouth was stuffed with a sock and tape was placed over the top. He couldn't move or scream, both things he desperately wanted to do at that exact time.

"Mr. Spivey," said Blue. "We are not going to hurt you, so don't worry. We are holding you for prisoner exchange. Your boss has someone we want back, and as soon as we get them, you can walk out of here as freely as you were a half hour ago."

The man nodded, but he did not look quite like he fully understood what was being said. The alcohol was having its way with him still. He shook his head to rid it of the cobwebs, but it did little good.

"If anything happens to my wife," interjected Logan, against the plan of the group. "If anything at all happens to her, then something will most definitely happen to you."

"We discussed this, Aster. We aren't here to hurt him. All we want is prisoner exchange. If they give up Janet, we give them Spivey."

"I don't want him to think this is as simple as you are making it, Blue."

"Oh, forgive me. Tying him to a chair and muting him is certain to make him think this is a joke."

"Fine, do it your way," said Logan. "I don't have to like it." He took out his phone and dialed the number he had for Nestor Jacobson. It rang several times before being picked up and it was indeed Jacobson who picked up on the other end.

"Aster! What a surprise. You know you can't hide well when you use the one device you can be tracked with."

"Let Janet got and you can have Spivey back."

"Spivey? You have my man?" asked the leader stunned but impressed.

"Yes, I have him. If you let my wife go, you can have him back with no other recourse. If you refuse, then he dies and then you die."

"Hold please…"

"What?"

On another phone, Logan could hear a ring, and then a man picked up and he wasn't sure what was happening until Jacobson spoke into the receiver of the second device. "Instead of taking them both, kill the old man. Aster wants to play hardball."

+++

Jaguar, the lead hunter on the mission to get Anisa and Able Lock, hung up the phone as soon as the boss had spoken. Sitting before him bound in the living room floor of the small house were the same two people he was there to find. Getting there had been easy since Anisa was still holding the pen her father had given her. It was clear to Jaguar and Komodo that Aster had no clue that it was a GPS tracking device that had been used to monitor his movements from the moment he left to go get his daughter from school. They could have gotten to him earlier and easier if there was not that damn twenty-four hour rule they had for tracking traitors to the group.

When they team entered the house, the initial goal had been to take Anisa and leave any witnesses behind unscathed. On the first of several hourly update reports, Komodo had learned from the team that there was an old man there who was acting as guardian for the girl. They were once again instructed to leave him unharmed but to tie him up so he could not go after them, if he in fact had a suicide wish. They had listened and tied him up, not harming a hair on his head in the process. The same could even be said for the girl, though there were no specific instructions when it came to her.

Now, the boss had called to change the game plan once again. He wanted the old man eliminated for what he said was Logan wanting to play games with them. He thought better of asking what that meant, but he knew he would have to follow through with the boss's wishes at the least. He took the old man by his shirt collar and stood him up. He was not as weak as he looked and he fought as much as he could with his hands tied.

Jaguar punched him in the jaw and sent him to his knees. He then placed a knee in his back and pushed him forward to the ground flat on his face. He knelt and put his knee into his back and put a not insignificant amount of his massive weight into it. "Stop struggling. You are making this worse for yourself. We don't wanna do it in front of the girl, but we will if you make us. So, stand up, come with me, and make this easy on us all."

"Fuck you! I am not making anything easy for you. If you are going to kill me, then it is going to be on my terms."

"No, I am afraid that's untrue." He pulled out his pistol and fired it into the old man's head, the bullet racing through the bone and brain and exiting into the wood floor on which he was sprawled. Anisa screamed, having seen the whole situation unfold.
Piranha and Grizzly grabbed the girl and carried her to the bedroom, each holding her up by one elbow. She kicked the air and got no leverage and went nowhere. She twisted and shook, again to no avail. "There is no rule against putting a bullet in your brain too, so I recommend you stop that," said Piranha in a deep, intimidating voice.

She stopped squirming and went willingly. She was unsure of what they had planned for her, but it could not be good if they were willing to kill Able to get her. It seemed at the start as if Able was as safe as she was, and then that phone call had altered everything, and now Able was dead and she was in the hands of the same enemy her dad had brought her there to avoid. She wished more than at any point in her life that her dad was there to protect her from these men.

CHAPTER SEVEN

It was a couple of long days later when the first package arrived. Logan knew immediately that they had gotten the location from him using the phone to contact Nestor Jacobson to tell him that they had Spivey. Logan knew that Jacobson now had Anisa too, so he had to play a much more cautious game going forward. He could not do anything that would put the lives of his wife or his daughter at more risk than he already had. The chances were high that both were in life-or-death situations, but it was impossible for Logan to know how long it would be before Jacobson decided that they had no more viable use and dispatched of them.

Red carried the box inside and placed in on the table in the kitchen. It was heavy, and Logan was almost afraid to open it. He slid the blade of the razor across the thick tape, slicing it a little at a time, each centimeter of cut tape equal to the unease he was feeling at the same time. When the whole thing was cut and ready to be opened, his unease was at its peak. He backed away and took a deep breath before he even considered popping open the top and looking inside. When he got comfortable enough, he did just that, and then leapt back in horror.

"The fuck is that?" asked Blue, who had also seen it when it was open.

"That's the head of the man who raised me," said Logan, feeling little emotion about the death of the man, but showing a lot for the fact that his death meant Anisa was in more danger than he feared.

"Care to repeat that?" asked Blue.

"A man, Able Lock, who took me in when I was a kid. He raised me and he was the one watching my daughter while I looked for her mother."

"Who the fuck did this then?" asked Red. "They must really have it in for you."

"Oh, that's an understatement. The man who did this wants me dead as badly as you do…or pretty damn close."

"What the fuck did you do to piss him off this much?" asked Blue.

"Simply put, I refused to kill my wife and daughter."

"What? He took a man's head and mailed it to you because you wouldn't kill your own family? And this is the asshole we are protecting you from?"

"You are not protecting me from him. You are helping me get back my wife…and now my child…from him and his organization."

"Okay, so this is what he is capable of. Who does this to a person who did nothing wrong to them? I mean, we kill people all the time, but they always have something in their past dealings with us that warrants it. Hell, I've even cut off a head or two in my day, but this is sick."

"Now you have an idea of why I came to you," said Logan. "I could never go toe-to-toe with them, get back Janet and Anisa, and survive to live out my life with them. I can take out the hunters, their elite squad, but I cannot take out the whole organization and do a recovery."

"Seems to me," said Red, "that you won't be able to do it without a lot of help, and I get now why you thought you needed it. The trouble is, no one is going to want to die for you. We hate you and we want you dead. The only reason we are here with you now is Torrance told us to come. When he finds out what he has put us up against, he is not going to want to continue with this deal."

"I couldn't care any less about who wants what. I want my wife and child back, and the only way to get them might be for you and your men to be in danger. The deal says I go free after this anyway, so why not just play nice?"

"Because," input Blue. "There is a dead man with his head in a box in your hideout who has done nothing to be dead. It is literally because of you that he is dead. If he will kill innocent men this way, then what the fuck is he likely to do to people who come after him with the goal of killing him?"

"He is going to kill people, that's what he does. He is dangerous, but so are we. We are not ruthless, so we have to be cunning. If he comes for us, we have to be ready. I took out one of them on a fucking airplane on my way to see you. I took out others at my house, twice. I had to protect my kid from gunfire. I don't care what it cost me or other people. I am bringing my baby girl home safely."

"You don't care what it costs? Well, we do. We aren't going to just sacrifice ourselves in the name of a man who betrayed us two decades ago and nearly ended us," said Blue.

"Yeah," said Red. "We nearly lost it all because you killed an important man. You didn't care about other people then and it seems like you don't give a fuck about them now. You can say you're changed or whatever because you have a family, but the truth is that you are the same asshole who killed a man without knowing what he meant to others."

"I was fourteen years old when I killed him. I had no idea who I was killing. All I was told was he was rich and if we killed him, we would also be rich. It wasn't untrue, but I understand now that I should have asked some more questions."

"That's what we are doing now. We are asking questions. Making sure it is worth our while to die fighting with the man who betrayed us. I know, you were young and you didn't understand, but does that somehow mean the rules didn't apply to you? Torrance thought so little about your age that he put out a hit on you. When he learned your age, he didn't rescind it. He said that he wanted it more than ever because he didn't like what you were destined to grow and become. He was right," said Blue.

"To top it off," said Red, "when you evaded us for so long, it became like a slap in the face. We wanted you dead so badly, but we didn't want to waste the little money we had chasing you. It was ironic that you killing the financier got the hit put on you but made us so vulnerable that we couldn't even go after you to ensure the hit was completed."

"I wasn't trying to do anything to hurt the cartel. I didn't know who you were or that you even existed. I killed a man I was ordered to kill and for reasons I was taught were noble. I don't apologize for killing him, and I never will. I can sit here and say I am sorry for what it caused your team. If I had known, even half of what I know now, I wouldn't have done it and caused the chaos I did."

"Apologies are nice and all, but there is a reason you work for us right now. You are proving to us that you can be trusted. The man whose head is in that box is family to you, and you don't even care. Why should we trust that when it comes time to keep us safe, you will even bat an eye about letting us go down with the ship?" asked Blue.

"You can trust me. If letting you die means Janet or Anisa die, then there is no fucking way I will let anything happen to you either."

"That's good enough for now, I guess," said Blue.

"Yeah, good enough for now," echoed Red.

Red and Blue spent the evening trying to get the location of Janet and Anisa out of the man they had captured, Spivey. He was reluctant to speak to them, and when they threatened genuine torture, he was a lot more willing to open his mouth about whatever they wanted to hear. He spilled information about the location, how many people were there, the size of the structure, and how many people it would likely take to storm it with success. He was forthcoming, but there was no way to verify it without going there for themselves and checking it out. Red stayed with Spivey and Blue went with Logan to the site Spivey had told them to find.

It was exactly as advertised. It was a concrete structure with no exterior windows. It was unlit and there were no bulbs anywhere that either of them could see. The only way in or out of the building was through a wooden door at the front. Spivey was right when he said it would be guarded by two men. They were standing on either side of the door. He had warned them that once inside, they would encounter about ten men before even getting to the prison cell door. There was no way for them to see inside, but with the accuracy of the other details, there was no reason to disbelieve this bit of information.

They took what they had learned and went back to the house. Spivey was still tied and Red and he were talking about some sporting even that had been on television recently. Logan was not a sports fan so it was a foreign language to him. He was still shocked to see someone as hardened as Red conversing with a prisoner they were using as leverage. It was not exactly breaking any rule, so he ignored it.

"Red, Blue, I need you to ask Torrance for more men. We need to raid that building, but there are too many men for just the three of us. I can easily take out the two guards on the outside, but there is no way to know the positions or weaponry of the men inside. If we break the door down and go guns blazing, we guarantee half of gets killed. If we plan it out, measure our steps, and take little risk, then we should be able to walk away with no loss of life and the two hostages."

"Okay," said Blue. "I will ask for them, but that means we cannot hit them until the day after tomorrow. We need to walk them through the plan and get everyone in position. If you are okay with waiting, then I am fine with asking for men. You have to promise me…us…that you will do everything in your power to keep everyone alive on this mission."

"You have my word, even though it is worth shit to you."

Torrance agreed to send ten men on a chartered flight to Washington, DC within the next two hours. They would arrive late that evening but would be at the disposal of Logan and work for him. Blue and Red agreed to do what Logan said as well, and when Torrance was told there were no problems thus far, he was pleased. He was still iffy on the prospect of working with the man he hated so much, but it was in his favor for the present time.

The men arrived and were given the rundown on the plan. There was only one thing left to do. Logan assigned each man a task according to his abilities, and the one woman, Pink, was going to be with him since she had training as a hitwoman in her native Ghashara. She had worked with the military and independently, much like Logan had done with his similar set of skills. She wasn't as good or as accurate as he was, but it would be nice to have a second barrel aimed at the guards just in case.

When all of the jobs were established and everyone knew their role perfectly, the only thing left was to wait.

When the time finally came, they departed in three jeeps that the men had driven from the airfield and arrived at the hidden recon location a few minutes later. Red was once again left to monitor Spivey, but he seemed okay with that. He had kind of bonded with the man in a way that a cartel assassin could with a mercenary who was working for a man that was likely going to be attempting to kill him before too long. Logan hated their bond, but he couldn't bring himself to say anything about it because everyone was sacrificing comfort for this job.

Once at the compound, after walking the few blocks to complete the journey, everyone took up their battle stations. Logan and Pink took their spots across from the main entrance and had a clear view through some trees of the guards who would never see them no matter how hard they might look in that direction. They both aimed rifles at the men, though the plan was for Logan to fire the kill shots for both. If he ran out of time and was in danger of not making the second, then Pink would intervene. Her secondary job was to put a hole through anyone who exited the doorway unless it was Anisa or Janet, both of whom she had pictures.

With radios in hand, all of the operatives relayed to Logan they were in place and ready to kick the raid into gear. Hearing this, he fired the first shot that entered the forehead of the guard on the left of the door. Before the other guard even had a chance to look over and see his partner dead, Logan fired a shot into his temple. With them both down, he radioed to the others to advance. They moved in while Pink held her position. Logan moved in with the others and two of the newcomers breached the door with a metal ram.

Three men stormed in with guns at the ready. They pointed their rifles in all directions, searching for anything moving or breathing. Those guards Spivey had told them about were nowhere to be seen, but Logan was not ready to call him a liar just yet. As they moved and more men entered, there were still no guards. Logan came in last and he immediately recognized that something was extremely wrong. All along the upper part of the walls was a balcony with a wall that rose up about three feet. He hardly had the chance to say anything when the first man stood from behind the barrier and fired a shot that missed its mark, but made its point.

"Fucking hide!" yelled Logan at the top of his voice to all of the men in the room with him. There was a total of eleven people and they all spread out in every direction, looking for whatever shelter there was from the barrage of bullets that suddenly floated down from above.

The sounds of shells striking everything from the concrete floor to the walls sounded like a war zone, but no one was being hit. Logan couldn't imagine that was the plan, but these guys were too good at what they did and they definitely would not want anyone walking away with knowledge of who they were or what they did. Logan rushed out and ran for the door that it made sense to him his wife would be behind. When he got to it, the men on the floor started finally returning fire to the balcony. It was enough to slow the bombardment, but the door did not budge for him. Logan worked on it and then shells hit the door around him. He wasn't sure who was shooting where, but his concentration was too broken to open the door by conventional means. He took out a metal spike he carried with him in case he needed something picked or unlocked, and stuck it in the keyhole. It was not an easy access port like a house door, but he managed to use it to align the plates and heard the audible click of the door giving way.

He threw it open and there in the middle of the room was a metal chair, but the room itself was empty. There was not a soul inside, and it made him furious. They had somehow known that he was coming and moved her to a new location. It would take pulling Spivey's teeth literally to get him to give up the information they needed now. It made sense why he was so giving with the details originally, and Logan hated himself momentarily for not seeing it when it mattered. He didn't enter the room. Instead he turned around and took aim at the men above him with reckless abandon.

He hit the wall of the barrier and the wall behind the men, but he was making them hide. All he wanted at this point was for his men to make it out of there and regroup, come back some other time, and finish what they had failed today. There was too much happening for Logan to see anything other than the place his own shots ended up, but when it felt right, he gave the order. "Evac, now!" he screamed. "Get out, get out, get out!" A parade of men ran for the door and then exited from it like they had been running from a giant snake. Logan came out right behind them, and they ran for the jeeps. Logan radioed to Pink to meet them there, which she did.

Logan was horrified to learn that two of the men had been killed in the gunfight. They were ones he had not met personally and didn't have any relationship with, but the people they had worked with for countless missions certainly knew him and would mourn him for a period. Logan was just saddened that he had not been able to get them all in and out with the ease and safety he had promised them. He had told them they would encounter problems, and possibly gunfire, but he didn't want to admit there was a chance people would die. Now, he just had to face that incredibly harsh reality because it had happened.

Back at the house, Logan explained what he had found in the room, apologized for getting men killed, and then asked everyone to leave so he could make some progress with Spivey. Red stayed and helped him interrogate the man, upset that Logan decided asking questions alone was not going to work any longer. "Where are they, you son of a bitch?"

"Who? What are you talking about?" asked Spivey.

"You told us what we wanted to know because you knew they had been moved. Where did Nestor move them to?"

"Who is Nestor?" asked Spivey seriously.

"Komodo!" screamed Logan. "Where did he move my wife and daughter to?"

"I don't know. I was sure they were at the dungeon. That's where he takes people when they have been captured."

"You're lying," said Logan and he struck the man in the face with the butt of his pistol. "You knew they were gone and that's why you volunteered the information so fucking easily."

Tears beginning to roll down his cheek, Spivey shook his head. "I didn't know. I swear. I thought I was helping you so I didn't get hurt."

"Don't lie to me," and he struck him again on the other side of his face.

"I am not lying," Spivey said, crying now. "I swear if I had known they weren't there, I would have said something."

"Enough," said Red. "I don't think he's lying, Aster. If he knew something, he would not have lied to us and risked being hurt, or tortured."

"I want to know where they are. Even if he didn't know," Logan said directly to Red, "I am guessing he does know the secondary location."

"Then ask him that and stop striking him."

"Just because he has become your new best buddy does not mean I give a fuck about him or what happens to him. I will do what it takes to find my wife and daughter. Don't like it, then get the hell out!"

"I am not gonna tell you how to do this. I am just saying that maybe this isn't the best way to approach it. He seems willing to tell you information to save his own ass, so ask him what you need to know and see what he gives you. Remember, his ass is on the line and he loves that thing."

Logan changed his approach and went back to simple questions that Spivey was quick to answer. He didn't reveal the actual location of the place where Anisa and Janet were likely being held, but he did give them what they needed in terms of where they wouldn't be. There was zero chance they were at the compound and that meant they would have to find someone who knew the inner workings of the organization to tell them, or better, take them to the place they needed to go. Spivey gave them exactly what they needed, in exchange for his own life. It was agreed that if any part of it was inaccurate, they would execute him and do the rest on their own. Since Spivey was terrified of dying, and he had said so several times, there was no reason to believe he had been lying about anything.

The next day, the team was gathered in the dining room, planning how they would use the new information from Spivey, when the doorbell rang and a delivery person was standing there with a tiny box. Since no one was expecting a package of any kind, Logan felt that unease creep back in that he had felt the last time a package had come to his door, that time with a head in it. This one was far too big for a body part like that, which almost made is scarier.

Logan answered the door and took the package into the dining room. The gathered masses sat silent as he walked in and placed the box down on the table. If it was as bad as he assumed it would be, they would have a clearer understanding of who they were dealing with. Red and Blue already knew. They hated that the man was so brutal and gruesome, but if the others knew and felt the same way, they might try harder to bring him to his knees.

With the box tape cut, Logan slowly pried the edges free. He could see red and that was never a good sign. He just hoped that it wasn't going to be an organ of some kind, though it would have taken some real force to fit it inside a box that size. When it was all the way opened, he audibly gasped. He stepped away from the table and almost fell down. Blue caught him and held him up on his feet. Inside the box was something almost worse than the head of the man who raised him. There were two things and neither led him to believe that Nestor was going to be sympathetic about the scenario. Logan stepped back to the table and stared down at the ring finger and wedding ring he had given Janet many years prior. Next to it was his daughter's index finger with the little fake ink tattoo she loved to wear on it of a heart with an arrow. There was no doubt in his mind that these were the real article and they did indeed belong to his wife and daughter.

"Aster, what the hell are we looking it at here, man?" asked Blue.

"Th-th-those are the fingers of my wife and daughter. Nestor is not playing softball. He is sending me a message. If this takes much longer, they will both be dead."

"Fuck this!" said one of the newcomers. "Whoever this guy is, he is crazy. I don't want any part of this."

"Shut the fuck up," said Red. "You are a part of it and you will be until it's finished or you die. You know, whichever comes first." The man didn't speak again after being rebuked in such a way.

"I hate that this is happening the way it is," said Blue. "It does paint a damn clear picture of who we are dealing with though. I don't think anyone in this room has any doubt that the man who would do that," and he pointed to the box on the table. "Would have any qualms about doing that or worse to people who are trying to stop him…or kill him."

"I agree," said another newcomer. "There is no question that the person we are working against is out of his fucking mind. I for one and ready to walk into wherever he is and lay an ass whooping he will never forget."

"While I understand that some of you are not happy with me, and don't want to be here helping me, I do appreciate that you are putting the animosity aside and doing what you are. I cannot guarantee that anyone else is not going to die fighting this battle, but I guarantee success in the long run."

"Don't listen to anyone saying that they don't want to be here. We are with you in this. You scratch our backs, we scratch yours." Red looked at the men he was familiar with. "You will do what we are here to do because it is an order. I am not telling you to like it, or even enjoy it for a single second. I am only telling you that as long as there is breath in your body, you will follow the orders to defend Logan, rescue his family, or anything else Blue, myself, or Torrance feels you need to be doing. Let me make it simpler for those who plan to make a retort: if you don't follow orders, you will be considered a traitor and suffer the consequences." He didn't say what those were, but the reactions on the faces of the men around the room said they knew exactly what Red was talking about and they didn't like hearing it.

"I need Red, Blue, Pink, and one volunteer with a verifiable ability to engage in hand-to-hand combat to stay in here with me. All the rest of you can go to the other room and hang out there for a bit. Keep an eye on Spivey every few minutes. Just peek in and make sure he is not causing problems. He is in the upstairs bedroom at the end of the hallway."

The one woman and four men, including the one who volunteered and went by the name Stryker, sat at the dining room table where the box no longer rested. Logan had put it in a safe place in his bedroom down the hall on the bottom floor. There were papers spread out all over the tabletop with drawings and diagrams. They had all been made by Red with the information Spivey had spilled to them previously. They were as detailed as one would expect in a few hours, but they would unquestionably assist greatly in their mission to find the next target.

"Okay," said Red. "Here is where the man upstairs said we could find Greyhound. It is a little shop outside of town. He deals drugs there according to Spivey, and we can find him there any day of the week. He operates out of there several hours per day."

"How about getting inside?" asked Blue. "Is it guarded or what?"

"No, getting in should be a piece of cake. It is a public shop. Once inside, though," said Red, "there is a back room that you will not so easily be able to access."

"Okay, so any tips for getting in there?" asked Pink. "If we can't just walk in and go get the guy, what's the plan?"

"Spivey said that coming with money and the phrase of the night will get you in," said Red. "The trouble we are gonna have is that we don't know the phrase and it isn't something Spivey can give us."

"So, we have to go in, mingle with the people, pick up the phrase intentionally or by accident, and then weasel our way into the back room?" asked Blue.

"Spivey said that once you are inside, there are enough people that there will be no attention paid to you by the staff," said Logan knowledgably.

"Then that's what we do," said Blue. "We go in, the new guy can mingle with the people, Pink can play seductress or whatever, and when they get the passphrase, they give it to us and we storm in."

"Sounds easy when you put it that way," said Red. "Does anything ever go that smoothly though? I think we need to be ready for all eventualities."

"Yes, it is unlikely it goes that well, so we are planning for alternatives. Pink will be the go-to if it goes south. She will grab Greyhound if he gets out of the back room and into the main servicing area," said Logan.

"Okay, but if he doesn't get free, all I am is the slut? Got it!" said Pink jokingly.

"So, everyone has and knows their roles," said Blue. "The only person who is in genuine danger here is Logan since he is going face-to-face with the target. The rest of us just need to be alert and ready to act if things take any kind of a turn."

They finished discussing the plan and then organized a time that fit everyone. After speaking to Spivey about it beforehand, they came to realize that midday was a better opportunity than early morning or late afternoon, so they were going to go after Greyhound at one the following afternoon. The group was prepared and the time couldn't come soon enough. Logan wanted nothing more than to walk away with him family safe and sound sooner rather than later.

CHAPTER EIGHT

After finishing lunch at the house the next afternoon, the five team members left for the small shop where their next target was said to be working a secondary or perhaps tertiary racket. Spivey was not specific about the look of the shop, but when it came into their view, they saw that it was only as small as a convenience store and there was nothing in the vicinity of it. It was dilapidated and unwelcoming. If anyone was inside, they likely had no respect for themselves. The windows on the front were covered with tape and slats of wood to conceal gaping holes. The glass was discolored and dingy. The entry door was glass and the only clean looking part of the whole structure.

Red parked the jeep in a spot in the lot so that it was impossible for someone to park next to him. On one side there was a huge dumpster and on the other a fence that was dividing the land from nothing, though there was something there once upon a time. The five of them hopped out and acted as much as possible as if they belonged there. No one would recognize them and that gave them the advantage they really needed.

Entering the shop itself, Logan realized what kind of shop it was, something that Spivey had been unable to tell them. They were a restaurant and lounge. Not quite a bar, but close enough that people would come to sit and have drinks. There were tables where men and women were playing cards and dice games. A waitress was walking around and handing out food and drinks to customers who had ordered them. Pink and Logan walked right up to the bar and sat on stools there. At the same time, the other three took spots at various empty chairs at random tables.

The gruff bartender behind the counter took orders from the two new customers and then all but threw their drinks down on the tabletop in front of them when they were made. They talked to each other as if they had known one another for their whole lives and no one was wise to their scam. The bartender never even tried to listen to what they were saying.

Meanwhile, the other three were sitting and drinking alone when one of them got a bite. A woman dropped her food on her seat and walked over to sit with Blue, who was extremely attractive for his age of 47. He still had a full head of dark hair and a goatee. His brown eyes were more of a pretty gold than the darker color a lot of people's were. He had a wonderful smile, though it was as fake as the breasts on the woman at the table with him. His white teeth were sparkling when he saw her. "Hi," he said as she sat down in the vacant chair.

"Hello, handsome," said the woman. "Mind if I have a seat?"

"Seems you're already sitting, might as well stay."

"Thanks," she said and rubbed his arm. "Can I get you anything to eat or drink?"

"Nah, I'm fine, but thanks anyway."

"What brings you here? Never seen you in here before."

"Hoping for some of the back room action. I need a fix and I was told this was the place. What brings you here?" asked Blue.

"Same. Greyhound has the best shit."

"That's what I hear." He smiled at the woman brightly. She smiled back at him. They continued talking and it was not long before the talented Blue (who had not needed to use his false name of Reginald Harrison) had turned the conversation toward the requirements for getting inside. More clever than most, he had asked her what passphrase she had to make sure he had the same and correct one, and when she spilled it easily due to a couple too many drinks, he nodded and said, "Yep, same one I have." She was too out of sorts to catch on and he walked up to the bar to tell Logan using a code of holding up three fingers when he ordered something.

Blue sat next to Logan and started chatting him up like they had just met, and again the barman ignored them. Somewhere along the line, Blue was able to tell him the passphrase and he stood up and walked, silently, to the door in the back, shrouded in darkness, and knocked.

"Who is it?" asked a voice from behind the door, peering through a mail slot that was abnormally high on the door.

"The devil went down to Georgia," said Logan, repeating the phrase Blue had uttered to him. He was waiting for the door to be opened while Blue and Pink were now standing directly behind him.

The door swung inward and Logan and Blue entered with no problem. This room was crowded to a degree the front room could never dream. Every table was filled to capacity and there more card games happening in here, but the stakes were higher. Each table had thousands if not tens of thousands of dollars visible on its top, and the people holding the cards were scary looking at best and utterly frightening and inhuman looking at worst. There were famous movie monsters that looked more approachable.

"I am looking for Greyhound," said Logan emphatically.

The man he was speaking to didn't say anything back, but instead pointed to a short, skinny man at a table in the corner of the room. He was doling out cards for a poker game and chatting with the men seated with him. Logan walked in his direction, but a large gorilla of a man stepped in front of him and placed a massive hand on his chest. "Nope, can't go there. Nobody sees Greyhound unless he asks for you."

Not sure what to do, Logan thought on the spot, and then said the first thing that came to mind. "I need what he's selling. I have money, I just need to speak with him."

"Fine, stay here and I will tell him." He walked away and came back just as quickly and shook his head in the negative. "He says you can fuck off and to leave the den." He took Logan by the shoulder and led him to the door, opened it, and pushed him out. Before the door shut behind him, he saw that Blue was still inside and might be their only hope of getting him on comfortable ground.

It was not long before Blue was expelled as well simply for coming in with the nosy bastard. There was only one choice left. They had to wait until he left and take more risks. They didn't know how long it was going to be before he left, so it became a waiting game. All five of them sat and drank, lingering until the moment their target exited the room they called the den and went to his vehicle. They didn't know which vehicle was his. No one seemed to.

Four long hours later, he walked out as if he owned the place and strolled across the floor to the exit. He was followed by the team, all of whom had every set of eyes in the place on them from the instant they stood up. When they got outside, Blue and Red nabbed him and dragged him to the jeep with a hand over his mouth and his feet trailing on the ground. Pink took the man's keys and she and the newcomer drove the car back to the house.

Blue, Red, and Logan were so busy that they didn't notice the group of men who left the building after them. They didn't go for the team members. Instead, they remained posted until the jeep took off and then chased them in their own vehicle, a small Toyota so that it was less conspicuous than one of the many expensive cars they could have chosen.

Logan was in the driver's seat of the jeep and Red informed him that they were being followed at first, and then it became a full-on pursuit. The jeep sped up to its quickest speed on the terrible dirt road outside of the shop. The Toyota did the same. When they hit paved road both vehicles accelerated to a massive degree, hitting speeds upwards of eighty. With the other traffic in the area, they were also weaving in and out, avoiding other cars and trucks all along the way. With close calls every few seconds, Logan was terrified, but there was no way he could stop. The men pursuing them wanted them dead, and they would do whatever it took to make that happen.

Speeding down a main road now, Logan found a hole in the traffic and put the pedal to the floor, jolting the jeep forward in such a way that it left the unsuspecting Toyota in its dust. When the driver spotted the jeep, he again copied the move and creeped ever closer to it. Within striking distance now, the driver of the car rammed the jeep in the rear bumper, pushing it forward and causing it to fishtail. Logan corrected it and lost speed while doing so.

The car was no side by side with the jeep and swung its passenger fender into the driver's door, again knocking it off its course, but this time it careened into the retaining wall that was in the middle of the road. Trying to correct at such high speeds, Logan easily overcorrected and jumped into the oncoming traffic on the other side of the road. The Toyota was keeping pace in the safety of the right lane, but the jeep was weaving among the cars coming right for it like they were making the world's largest and most dangerous woven basket. Horns blared and lights flashed, but there was nowhere for the jeep to go except straight.

The Toyota was moving along at the same speed, and suddenly Logan made the brash decision to leap back into the other lane. He jerked the wheel to the left and the jeep jumped as if it were on a ramp and slammed into the Toyota, knocking it into the wall and sending it spinning. Now out of control the Toyota was hitting cars left and right, while more horns and lights attempted to quell the chaos. After slamming into several vehicles and finally righting itself, the Toyota was once again able to track the jeep, which was a speck in front of it at this point. Word had spread and the traffic ahead had left the road in a desperate attempt to stay alive and unharmed. The Toyota took the opportunity and raced forward, catching up with the jeep a short time later. Both vehicles were running top speed in a straight line, the Toyota weaving toward the jeep occasionally to scare the driver, but doing so unsuccessfully.

They both took the off ramp toward the city when it came up. They had to slow down significantly, and this gave them a chance to regroup and get full control of their respective vehicles and situations. Logan rode the middle of the small road and the Toyota rode more on the right side. The left fender of the Toyota was even with the right fender of the jeep. They sped along at reduced speeds from those on the main road, and when Logan saw an opening, he hit the gas and once again left the Toyota to stare at where it had been.

Logan, seeing that he had gotten rid of the pesky car for the time being, stopped the jeep and all four men got out, Greyhound less willingly than the others. The only building nearby where they could run was a school and there were hundreds of students out in the courtyard of the grounds. He hated the idea of putting the kids in danger, but he and the men needed to get away from the tail.

They took off into the courtyard with their weapons, trying their best to hide them. Their ruse fell apart quickly when one of the teachers spotted them and screamed! "Everyone inside, shooters on the grounds!"

There was no way to say they were anything else and it was going to take quite a while for them to explain they were there because they too were running from shooters. The kids all scrambled back into the building and the three of them were left unguarded in the soccer field. It wasn't long before the police sirens could be heard in the distance and the last thing they needed was to be caught on school property with semi-automatic weapons. When the Toyota never showed and the men didn't come with guns of their own blazing, Logan and the others ran back to the jeep and took off just in time to avoid the police parade that had shown up far too long to do anything if the situation had been real.

At the house, Logan and Blue tied the man to a post in the basement and Red carried down a bag filled with utensils that would be used to extract the relevant information. If Spivey was being honest (he was going to be in the room to watch as a tactic) then Greyhound had been through his fair share of situations in which he had been tortured to some extent. Logan was not expecting him to just spit out what he wanted to hear, but he also hoped it didn't go too far since he was about as inexperienced in torture as anyone. Red and Blue both told him they had no experience with it either. There were specialists within Diamond for that sort of stuff.

After everything was prepped, Red went up to get Spivey and drug him down to the party. He was seated in a wooden chair and tied up there. He was told to keep a close eye on what was happening to Greyhound because if he lied or didn't give them what they needed, he was next. His fear was evident and his heartrate had intensified. He knew what was coming but he didn't know what methods Logan was planning to use.

"I swear I never lied. He can withstand a lot, but he knows what you want to know. I guarantee it," said Spivey, nearly pissing himself in terror.

"He better," was Logan's simple reply.

With the man tied to the post, Red took out a small knife from the bag and handed it over to Logan who took it gleefully. It was not supposed to entice those kinds of reactions when you were planning on forcefully ripping information from people, but Logan was long past caring about what was normal. He placed it on the man's inner thigh and slowly slid it across the tough muscle. It created what amounted to a paper-cut sized streak of blood. The man squealed a bit in pain, but it was short lived.

"Tell him what he wants to know, or there will be 999 more of those!" said Blue seriously.

'I have no idea what you want to know," grunted Greyhound.

"Where are Janet and Anisa Aster being held?" asked Logan.

"Who? I don't even know who that is!" said the man angrily.

Logan cut him four more times on his ankle, calf, and thigh. With all three wounds pooling blood on his legs, Greyhound was in obvious agony. He wasn't speaking, but Logan was far from being finished with him. He asked again and got nothing, so he cut again, this one in his gut and much deeper. He gagged from the pain, but he didn't talk.

"Tell us and this all stops," said Blue. "It really is that easy."

"If I tell you anything, I am dead anyway, so you may as well go ahead and finish me off."

"No, it is not going to be that easy," said Red, surprising everyone in the room. "We aren't gonna kill you if you don't tell us. We know everyone has a price…and a limit. We will find yours, motherfucker!"

"Even if I knew, I wouldn't tell you. I would rather die with my mouth shut than die a traitor to the people I work for."

"You are a smart man," said Logan, "but, you're also a dumbass. If they find out you were here, you are dead whether you talk or not. I can offer you freedom if you talk, and you can even run and hide. I don't give a shit what happens to you as long as you tell me what I need to know."

"It's gonna take a shitload more than that to convince me to give up a secret location for one of the most dangerous people on earth," said Greyhound. "If you think you have it in you, I say bring it."

Logan went at him hard, cutting his flesh over and over again and getting nothing from him. The next step was a little more gruesome, but Logan was running out of time in his mind. Seeing his wife and daughter's fingers had made him more than aware that they were in immediate danger of loss of life. He was ready to kill for answers, but the irony was that he would never get them if he killed the man in front of him. He could always try again with a new name, but that would be wasting more and more time that was certain he no longer had. For him, it was now or never, and never was definitely not an option.

The pitcher was too hot to touch anything on but the handle and even that was heating up by the second. The boiling water inside sloshed as Logan carried it to the spot where the man was now bound to a chair tightly. He squirmed when he saw the steam, but he couldn't have guessed how Logan planned to use it to his advantage. He inched closer and Greyhound tried to move away to no avail. He couldn't move in any direction and the more he tried, the tighter the ropes became. Red and Blue were great with knots, and the ones they had tied ably held the man and grew in tightness with tension applied, such as pulling away. Logan dripped a little bit on the man's leg and he screamed. The hot water melted away flesh like it was hot butter. He dripped a little more and the man screamed again. Bubbles were forming where the water was applied. Logan wiped with his hand and layers of skin came away like they were never attached. The man was shaking, but he still wasn't talking. Logan dripped some on the man's chest and he yelled like he had been shot. He was freaking out, but he refused to say anything. "This thing is full and those are small droplets. I have time and I am angry! It's up to you how much of this you get."

"I won't talk. I already told you that. Why do you insist on trying to make me? It isn't going to work," said Greyhound.

"That isn't going to keep us from trying," interjected Blue. "You saying it won't work is not the same as us knowing it will not work."

Logan poured a larger amount on the man's right hand. It sizzled as it burned the flesh and the man screamed in agony like Logan had never heard. He wanted badly to blow on it, to shake it for relief, but neither of those things was possible. He did the same thing quickly to the left hand, and the same reaction ensued. Red and Blue watched in amazement as the man let the pain subside and then pretended like nothing had happened.

"It's painful, sure. I can take it. I'm still not going to talk, so you can kill me any time."

"I don't plan to kill you just yet. My plan is to do a little more before I concede that you won't talk to us. You will know when I am ready to give up. I will walk up to you with an axe, and that will be the last thing you ever fucking see!"

"I look forward to what's in store, then," he said with a smirk.

Logan poured boiling water in as many places as he could think of that might have led the man to talk, but it did no good. He wasn't going to say anything with these amateur methods of torture. Logan knew that he was going to have to step up his game, and he had the best and worst idea at the same time. He was convinced it would work, but it was going to be messy.

Taking out a large carving knife, Logan walked wordlessly over to the man and stuck the point of it deep into the flesh of his leg. It was tough to get it through the muscle and tissue, but with more pressure, it went with ease. The man clenched his teeth and grunted in pain, but he didn't scream as he had done so many other times. Logan rolled his eyes, angered and exasperated by the whole ordeal.

Using the knife, Logan carved a small square of meat from Greyhound's thigh. Blood spewed and poured into the floor. He had tears in his eyes, but again he kept from yelling out. Logan cut more from various places and eventually, he made the move he knew would be the winner or ultimate loser of the whole day. Kneeling down to his naked midsection, he placed the serrated edge of the knife on the man's scrotum. He sliced a little and the man screamed. He pressed harder and the man kicked out nearly toppling the chair. "Last chance, you sick motherfucker! You talk or I cut off your dick and feed it to you!" yelled Logan furiously.

"No! Don't!" screamed Greyhound. "Jesus fucking Christ! I will talk! Just leave my cock alone!"

"Then talk, asshole! We are waiting," said Red. He had lost his patience with everything as much as anyone else had.

"This knife doesn't move until I know exactly where my wife and daughter are. Do you understand that?" asked Logan.

"Yes, I get it," said Greyhound. "They are at Melhoff Manor. It is a bunker in Maryland."

"I am gonna need more than that," said Logan as he slowly sliced a little more."

"Oww," yelled Greyhound. "It is in Trinity, right on the water…Lake Freedom. It is a concrete two story house. It is the only house made of concrete anywhere in the area."

"You don't have an address?" asked Blue, the only one somewhat calm in the room.

"No, there is no address. According to the state database, the place doesn't exist. It is as off-grid as you can get. All of the utilities are illegal and there is no record of a building or permits for one."

"How do we approach it?" asked Logan without looking up.

"You cannot get there without detection. It is impossible. There are sensors everywhere from the edge of the lake all the way to the house and beyond. If you walk on one, there are men trained to attack."

"How to we avoid the sensors?" asked Blue.

"You can't," came the voice that until now gone unheard. "There is no way to avoid them. Once you are in the area, they will find you and the men will attack and kill you." Spivey looked petrified, and Logan looked like he wanted to rip his head from his shoulders.

"You knew the whole fucking time?" asked Logan.

"No," said Spivey. "I know about the place, but I had no clue that's where they were."

Logan and Blue kept up with the questions, now including Spivey as well. Once they had what they needed, Logan untied Greyhound as promised. He was standing up from the chair and walking toward the stairs when Red pulled a small pistol from his belt and fired two shots into the back of the man's head. He lurched forward and then fell to the ground dead. Before anyone could stop him, he did the same thing to Spivey, firing twice into the man's chest, and then once in the forehead. He was dead before the second shot was fired. Logan lunged for Red but it was far too late.

"What the fuck did you just do?" asked Blue. "We made those men a promise and they kept their word."

"Yes, but there was no fucking way they were gonna walk away from here and not have your names on the tips of their tongues when they got where they were going. You were in as much danger as they were," said Red.

"One thing we don't do in the Diamond is betray people, and we don't lie about keeping promises. You know that. Betrayal has a consequence, remember that." As quickly as lightning strikes in a storm, Blue withdrew a pistol of his own and fired a shot through Red's head, killing him.

Logan looked at Blue, stunned into silence. He had killed his own friend and partner because he had done something that couldn't be forgiven by the organization for which they worked. As if nothing had occurred at all, Blue holstered the gun and walked up the stairs. Logan was left staring at three corpses in his basement where there should have been none. No one was supposed to die. That was never the goal of this exercise. It was only to get the information they had needed, and it worked for that.

As Logan traipsed back upstairs, he was met with the angry faces of the Diamond members who blamed him for it coming to Red losing his life. Blue took responsibility, but with the hatred that already existed for Logan among the men, giving them a reason for it was all the tinder this fire needed. The group was becoming fractured and that was going to make it damn near impossible to work together going forward. Logan didn't know how to wet the kindling, but if he didn't find a way soon, his wife and child would be dead and there would be absolutely no way for him to live with himself if that happened. "He is dead because he betrayed what your organization stands for. Don't blame me, don't look at me like I did this. No one made him kill two innocent men. The person responsible for his death is him. We have a job to do, and like it or not, that is what we are going to do."

Blue turned and pulled out his pistol again, this time pointing it at an unsuspicious Logan with his finger pressed firmly on trigger. "Not any more we don't! This ends here!"

CHAPTER NINE

Logan was able to finally diffuse the tension in the kitchen by talking to the gathered crowd and telling them they could do what they wanted to him when it was all over since once again they felt betrayed by him, but until that time came, they did have a job to do and if it didn't get done, they were all not honoring their agreement with him and therefore subject to the consequences. He took out his own pistol and pointed it at Blue who still had his own sighted on Logan. "I will start right here and move down the line. I will kill every fucking one of you if you back out on me. My wife and daughter will be dead for sure, so I will have nothing left to lose." He cocked the gun and let everyone know how serious he was. To everyone's shock, Pink also pointed a pistol at Blue's head.

"Alright, Aster," said Blue in surrender. "I am putting my piece away and I would appreciate if you would do the same." He looked at Pink with a glare that could kill and motioned for her to lower hers as well, and she complied as she saw Logan doing it.

"Are we all clear on what our objective is?" asked Logan.

Everyone nodded their assent and Logan walked over and pushed a couple people out of the way and sat down at the table. He dropped his head to the tabletop and groaned. He was exhausted from everything that had happened and what was still to come was weighing on him more than anything else. He pictured in his head the nightmare of doing recon, possibly getting caught or killed, then going back again to infiltrate, attempt a rescue, run away still hoping to be alive. It all added up and it was all stressful alone, but when put together as a whole, it was migraine-inducing.

When everyone and everything was back to a semblance of normalcy, and he had a break to do some research on the internet about motion sensors, Logan broke into a diatribe about what was coming next. The few who were left from Diamond, including Blue, Pink, and several newcomers, listened intently as Logan laid out a plan for doing recon on the Manor in Maryland. None of them had ever been to the area

Greyhound had described, and having only the words of a now-dead man to go by, there was no guarantee of any kind that they weren't walking into an elaborate trap.

"There is no way to actually avoid being detected. I did some research and he wasn't lying about that part. We are going to have to trick the sensors into believing it has been tripped by something else and not show ourselves until we have cover."

"Who is going on the recon?" asked Blue. "I am, you have no say. Pink is because she is the best shot out of all of us other than you. Who else?"

"Always five of us. Since Red is no longer part of the squad, it will be me, Blue, Pink, Stryker, and Doberman. You have roles that we will discuss when this is over. The others of you are here until we get back. What you do is your business. For the incursion, we will all be going." With Red dead, two men gunned down on the first attempt to get Janet back, Blue, Pink, and Stryker with him that left only the six who would be able to assist on the big mission when the time came. Logan was not positive it would be enough, so he hoped the reputations of the men and their abilities were not overhyped.

The members who were leaving were given detailed instructions on their roles and warned that any deviation from them could and likely would result in a gunfight at the least, and at worst the death of some of the men. Meant only as a tactic to scare them into wanting to do it right, Logan also knew that it was one hundred percent accurate. They were not going against high school kids with BB guns. These were highly trained professional fighters and killers. When the time came to vacate the house and embark on the journey to Maryland, they all left with the same feeling: it will not be me that causes people to die today.

The rented boat was heading for the edge of the lake, but there was no way without being there that Logan could know he had taken them in the right direction. He was thrilled when he saw the concrete standing resolute above the shoreline. He knew he was in the right place, and he also understood that he could not take them too close or they would be spotted, and likely shot and killed. He had an idea of where he wanted to anchor the boat so they could dive and swim to shore.

With it rocking gently in the water, they all alighted and dove beneath the surface. They swam in the direction of the land and kept a lookout for sensors as they went. Seeing nothing, they continued on their route. Tripping nothing along the way, they were shocked to see that no one was outside ready to put a bullet through their hearts when they emerged. Blue tried to climb out of the water without warning the others and that was when they heard an alarm, quiet from their vantage point, sounding in the house. Seconds later, there were men outside with guns drawn and aimed. Blue had made it back into the lake before they showed themselves. As they hoped, Greyhound was honest about there being no cameras and when the men checked on the sensors, they didn't seem too stunned that there was nothing. It was clearly something they had dealt with countless times before.

When the men went back inside, they tried the same tactic two more times. Replication was the key to knowing results were verifiable, valid, and reliable. All three times, the same thing occurred, so it stood to reason that it was an accurate representation of what to expect. Their reaction times were still too fast to risk moving on land when the alarm sounded, but they were getting slower out of boredom and repetition. After a few more tries, they stopped checking it out altogether and that was when they made their move to land.

They had to be swift or the alarm would last longer than it had before and curiosity would rear its head and the guards would come back out and see what was happening. Logan took the lead, guiding the team to the retaining wall on the edge of the property at the south. They all ducked behind it, waiting for the right time to peek and make notes of what they were seeing.

The first thing they needed to know was the reaction time for sensors in certain areas. They knew the one for the water and back yard. They needed to know how long they had if they activated the ones in each quadrant: north, south, east, and west. The only way to know was to activate them, so like little kids they picked up rocks and tossed them into the various areas. Counting the time for each reaction, they had a solid idea of how long they would have no matter where they breached.

They noted information for other vital aspects of the breach as well, such as distance to the house from certain points, difference in number of respondents to an alarm in an area, types and numbers of visible weaponry, and locations of entry and exit points to both the house and the land itself.

Having all of the information they needed, they prepared to dart back to the water and swim to the waiting boat. On Logan's count, they ran as fast as they could. The alarms tripped as they ran and the response was lightning quick. Everyone made it to the water's edge, and one of them tripped as he attempted to dive. The shot rang out and it was obviously a kill shot. It ran through the scuba suit, lodging itself in his lung. Two more were fired in quick succession with one hitting him in the upper back and the other piercing his cerebellum through the back of his head, killing him instantly. Logan didn't notice Stryker wasn't with them until he was doing a count on the boat before leaving. He, and the others looked back and saw his body half in-half out of the water, clearly deceased.

When the whole team returned including those left behind for the recon, there was no sign of Stryker. The blood and body were both gone as if he had never been there at all. It was a reminder to Logan being here again so soon afterward that these people were not afraid to exert their dominance and power by killing those who would trespass on their turf for any reason. They didn't hesitate to blow three holes into Stryker without knowing a damn thing about him. The danger was real, and now there were twice as many targets as before, so it was amplified by that much.

The boat anchored in nearly the same spot as before, everyone debarked and submerged themselves. The swim felt longer this time since they were trying to move a larger group and also keep an eye on a larger swath of area for sensors or worse. As they moved with the current, they saw nothing out of the ordinary. Arriving at the shoreline, they waited as instructed. "No one moves until my say-so," said Logan.

When the time came, they leapt from the water and darted to all four corners, predesignated by a joint council of Logan and Blue who understood the timing required and the speed of each man on foot. They should have had zero trouble reaching their stations based on the calculations that had been made for them. Logan didn't have a lot of time to think about it since he too was in the process of running to his established battle post.

Right on cue, the guards exited from all of the doors and saw nothing to alert them to the danger lurking in the shadows. As they stared around the property, there was no sense of doom; that is until Logan fired the shot that took down his guard. The other seven of them went down quickly as his shot was the cue for the others to fire on theirs. The ones who had not fired were responsible for breaching the door. That included all newcomers, and they made it without incident. Once the door was opened, Blue, Pink, and Logan moved into their positions to be the first through it.

Logan went before the others, followed closely by Pink and then Blue. When they were inside, there was no one in the large room, so they moved in further. As they did, the rest of the team entered and with all of them in the room, they broke into teams. There were five team of two each and they all took different rooms and searched. When anyone was spotted, they were to shoot without waiting for a reason. Logan told them they were looking for his wife, but he understood if something unfortunate happened to her with the order they were given. They didn't buy it for a second, but they listened to him. "Move in slowly. Remember, when you see anyone, you take them out. They are not gonna wait for you to ask questions or answer theirs."

The first round of blasts came from a room off to the left that Pink and Pryde had entered. They knocked the door down and immediately let loose. There was more to Logan's right when Hydra and Doberman found soldiers lying in wait. It wasn't long before the fight came to them.

Having heard the ruckus, there were now more than a dozen men armed to the teeth in the living room firing in all directions. Logan heard screams but he wasn't sure and couldn't check to see who they belonged to. He prayed silently that they weren't his men. By the time he could wrap his head around how much was happening, he was required to defend himself against an onslaught as a trio of soldiers came up on him and attacked him hand-to-hand. They had spent their cartridges and this was all they had left. Logan holstered his pistol and dropped the rifle and welcomed the challenge.

He was not in a movie and the men were not going at him one at a time. He was struck from three sides at once as one man kicked him in the back of the knee, one punched him in the jaw, and another in the gut. He was on the ground before he knew he had been hit that many times. He rolled and pushed himself to his feet but he was met by a knee to his ribcage that sent him falling to the side. Trying again to stand, he was hit this time twice with two feet into his lower back. One of the feet rested there and then the man stood on him like a stool. Not knowing the strength and determination of their opponent, they underestimated what he was capable of. Logan rotated his body and brought a knee into the groin of the man above him. He then granted him a foot to the face as he kicked himself to his feet like a martial artist.

He had no more than reached his feet again when one of the men clocked him in the jaw. He took the hit this time, absorbing it and retaliating with fury. He punched the man so hard that he nearly flipped. Able to stand fully up and regain his center, all three men were now fighting a wall of a man. He took them all three at once when he gripped the fist coming for his face and stomped the knee of the leg making its way toward his ribs. At the same time, he evaded the swing from behind with a duck that resulted in the man he was holding bearing the brunt of the force from the punch. Feeling tired and out of sorts, Logan decided it was time to cheat and win. He un-holstered the pistol and in fast sequence fired a bullet into the head of each man. The fight was over and he smiled despite himself. It was a war zone and he wore a grin like a badge of honor.

The fighting wore on with the others. There were bodies strewn all over the floor at with a glance, Logan knew some of them were of his men. He hated the recognition of the fact, but it remained that: a fact. He took the chance he had provided for himself to search rooms while the battle raged. He found nothing downstairs and ran upstairs. It was, of course, in the last room he checked that he found what he was looking for. There in the center of the room, guarded by two beasts for men, was Janet with a beaten and broken face, bruises from head to toe, and skin missing in several places. He saw the spot where her ring and finger used to be and wanted to kill the men with his bare hands. He couldn't do that, though. He pulled his pistol, fired it, and realized too late that it was empty. He had failed the simple task of counting shots to know when to reload, and now he was standing before two men who had weapons when he didn't. He ran into the room and dove for the first man. He hit him like a spear and sent him toppling. He hit his head on the window and was dazed enough that Logan could swing around and grab the neck of the second man and snap it like a dry twig. As the other man came to, Logan did the same to him. With both men dead, he untied Janet and helped her to her feet. She didn't speak, didn't hug Logan, didn't even look at him. Instead, she ran from the room, through the hallway, down the stairs, and out of the house without looking back.

Logan ran back down and into the fray. It was still an intense contest, but he yelled at the top of his lungs in an effort to reach all his men at once. "Mission abort! Fall out!" He made for the exit and everyone followed. When they all got out, he, Pink, and Blue walked back in with automatic rifles trained on the remaining enemy. "We will have those," Logan said, pointing to the weapons. All of the men surrendered their arms and the team walked away toward the water, except for Logan and Blue who tied up the ones left. When they finished, they too fled the house.

They leapt back into the water, four men short, and swam for the boat. They swam in pairs with Logan and Blue bringing up the rear. Logan heard the sound before he saw what was making it. He had only enough time to warn Blue and grab Pink before the device hit the small craft and exploded. Somehow one of the men had escaped his bindings and was standing on the shore with an RPG poised on his shoulder and a smile on his face. \Logan, Pink, and Blue were under the water, avoiding successfully the intense blast of the incendiary projectile. When the initial intensity vanished, they surfaced to find the boat in shards and the three people who had been on it nowhere to be found. There was almost no chance they were alive, and Logan hated that he had not just killed all of the soldiers in that house.

"Aster, what the fuck just happened?" asked Blue. "We tied those motherfuckers up before we left."

"I don't know," admitted Logan. "I have no idea. I know they were tied well, but maybe we missed one."

"That's a fair guess," said Pink, wiping a tear from her face. "Either that or someone betrayed us."

"We can't go there," said Logan. "I am confident no one went behind our backs to help the enemy." The words were hardly out of his mouth when through the smoke of the smoldering craft he saw a shadow on the shore that didn't belong to the shooter. So, there were at least two of them free out there.

"What do we do now?" asked Blue, a million thoughts racing through his mind. The most prominent one was about how they were going to ever make it home with their boat in literal ruins on the lake bottom.

"We have to swim to the dock. I know, it's a long way, but we have no choice. If we go slowly enough, they will not be there waiting for us. There is a chance they didn't see us after the explosion, so we might be in the clear."

"Where do we go when we make it back?" asked Pink. "If we are free and clear, shouldn't we go after them?"

"No, we can't reveal ourselves like that. If they think we are dead, we need to play that illusion, at least for a while," said Logan.

"Good point," said Blue. "We can gain the upper hand if we let them think we are dead. The problem is they will come looking to make sure they got us all. When they don't find all of us in the water, they are going to know."

"That could take days if not longer," said Logan. "We have time. As for now, we swim out, go to the house and regroup."

"Um, where is your wife?" asked Pink, wondering aloud what they were all thinking.

"I don't know," said Logan. "She wasn't inside the house." His lie was bought since no one had been paying enough attention to see a woman streaking away from the chaos. "We will have to keep looking for her. I only hope they mutilate her any further. I feel bad enough as it is."

In unison, as if they shared one thought process, Pink and Blue asked the same question in the same inflection and with the same curiosity. "Where do we look?"

CHAPTER TEN

With the incursion being a failure ultimately, either due to the loss of soldiers or the failure to retrieve Janet from the clutches of the enemy, Logan was feeling as down as he ever had. They had swam the lake to the dock where they were able to work their way back to the house. With only three people left to fight, Logan was losing hope in a way he never had before. He genuinely believed that Janet and Anisa were going to die. He was still curious why Janet had run off like that, but more so he was concerned because Anisa was not in the house at all. That meant Janet and Anisa were being held separately and it would be nearly impossible to find them both before an unknown timeline expired.

All three of them slept late the following day. The excitement had taken a major toll on them, and there was no room for more in the near future. The youngest among them was Pink and she was 31. It went without saying that they were too old for shit like this. Logan leapt out of bed when he heard the doorbell. He wasn't expecting mail, so his mind went to that dark place. He opened the door with a pistol at the ready.

"Package for Logan Aster," said the young boy with the small box, not unlike the other he had recently received, proffered.

"That's me," said Logan as he massaged the trigger of the gun behind the half-open door. "Any idea what it is or who it's from?"

"No clue, dude. I am just the delivery guy."

"Thanks," said Logan as he took it from the boy's hands and shut the door without another word. He took it to the kitchen table and opened it quickly. He was beyond the hurt that came from seeing the things Nestor was willing to send him in boxes, so he wanted to rip off the bandage fast and get it over with. Flipping the flaps aside, he stared down. What he saw was worse than anything he had imagined. It was his daughter's, he was sure. He and Janet had given those diamonds to her when she turned ten. She was allowed to wear them when she turned twelve. Seeing it still piercing the ear where it had always been word, the ear not attached to his daughter's head, made his stomach turn and he fought back the urge to vomit. "Goddamn it, you motherfucker!" he yelled.

His attitude had gotten the attention of Blue and Pink and they came running to learn the horrifying truth of what Logan had just discovered. Blue looked into the box and recoiled. He looked again because he had seen something. He reached in, and Logan grabbed his hand. "Don't touch it," said Logan.

"There is something in here. A piece of paper or something." Blue pulled it out and handed it to Logan who unfolded it and cringed. There was a note written, thankfully in plain ink, that gave an address that wasn't really an address at all and simply a street name in California, and a message: meet "home" noon Friday. If you aren't here, she dies."

"Son of a bitch! We need to get men and go there."

"Oh, fuck no!" said Blue. "Torrance will not authorize any more men. He already said as much. I mean, I can call him and ask."

"Please do," said Logan coldly while crumbling the paper in his sweaty palm.

Blue went to a different room to make the call. He came back looking dejected and Logan knew already what he was going to say. He was disappointed in the message but he was not surprised by it. He shook his head and began to wonder how three men were going to be able to take on a virtual army.

"I am going, even if it is only me. I refuse to let my daughter die just because I didn't feel like I had enough men to mount a rescue for her."

"You have me too," said Pink. "I am with you to the very end of this."

"You got me too, Aster. I will not be the reason a little girl dies if I can help it."

"I appreciate it, I really do," he said. "You need to understand that we are walking into an army with three soldiers of our own. We won't win this battle, and we are going for only one reason: Anisa."

"We know, Aster. I don't care anymore. Those fuckers have killed a lot of my friends and people I have done countless missions with. I want them dead as much as you do now," said Blue.

"Yeah, I second that," said Pink. "We are avenging our own as much as we are helping you get your daughter back."

"It won't be easy, and we won't have a plan like before. I only know the property from my one visit there to drop off Anisa with her grandfather."

"We can use what you know, I am sure it's sufficient for our needs."

"I trust you," said Pink with a small smile.

"Then we have some planning to do."

The doorbell rang again the following morning, but this time, Logan made no effort to answer it. After it rang several more times, he got the idea. It was a delivery person since they would not lose their cool and repeatedly press the little button that made the unholy ringing inside the house. He climbed out of his bed and made it to the front door. He could see a shadow through the curtain on the window and when he threw the door open, he was stunned to see the man standing there. He took a step back and let him inside.

"Torrance? What are you doing here?" asked Logan.

"I spoke to Blue yesterday morning. He told me you were having some problems with the man who took your wife, and apparently now your kid too. I sympathized with that part. It wasn't what drew me here."

"Care to tell me what did then?"

"Oh, that's easy. That motherfucker has killed a lot of my men. I want to be the one, as much as you do, to deliver the blow that ends his miserable fucking life."

"We might have to fight for that honor," said Logan with a wry smile.

"For that privilege, I would make you wish you were never born. Trust me."

Blue and Pink had heard the commotion and come down to see what was happening. They were both shocked to see their boss in the living room talking with Logan. Blue had told him what was going on and about the deaths of their men, but Torrance had never given any indications that he was coming to them. Blue couldn't even figure out how the man knew where to find them. Perhaps Logan wasn't hiding quite as well as he thought he was.

"Why are you here, boss?" asked Blue.

"I came to help. Those were my men that they killed. I paid them, I ordered them, and I sent them here to die. I want revenge as much as anyone else."

"Do you really think it's a good idea to put yourself at risk like that, da...boss?" asked Pink. The word had gotten far enough out of her mouth that Torrance rebuked her, but it wasn't heard by the two men standing near her, or at least they hadn't let on that they had heard anything out of the ordinary.

"If my men were willing to risk, or even give their lives for something, then I am not too good to do the same." He looked at Logan. "I assume you have a plan?"

"Yeah, we worked it all out last night. We move tomorrow and act Friday according to the note he sent. I will go alone first and meet with him. You come in after and prepare to engage. It is a nearly empty street and it would take police forever to arrive. The fewer shots the better, but there is no telling how many men he has inside."

"Sounds like a plan," said Torrance. "I can get the details from Blue and Pink."

Friday morning came and Logan drove from Los Angeles to Holbrook Desert a couple hour away. He couldn't get Anisa off his mind. He thought about the moment he learned she was going to become part of his life and just how little he cared and how poorly he responded. It was impossible to believe he would or could ever love anyone as much as he did Anisa from the moment she was born.

The hospital room was smaller than some he had been in, but that wasn't the reason he was there. He could have been in a cardboard box as long as the baby came out healthy and happy. He always dreamed of a smiling newborn when it first saw him. He was told that only happened in the movies, but he could hope for anything. The hours of labor for Janet and waiting for him paid off. Their little girl was born and when the doctor placed her in his arms for the first time, he shed a tear that would be one of many. He stared into the face that looked just like her mother and watched her little baby movements. He loved the little sounds she made. He loved her.

She spoke her first word, "mama," at age nine months. Logan hated that it wasn't his name, but he would never say anything to anyone about it. He was just happy and impressed that his baby had begun speaking. It wasn't long and speaking a word or two became speaking in sentences. She could hold a conversation by age three, and the words never stopped once she learned them and how to use them.

The time passed fast and it was already time for her first birthday. Janet and he had planned an elaborate party and invited people they knew with kids to come hang out. Only a few came, but they expected as much. They weren't close with anyone really. It was more about the thrill of it all than anything else. Anisa sat in her highchair and Logan put a small chocolate cupcake with chocolate filling and chocolate icing on the tray and let her have her way with it. She had dug into it like she had never had sweets before. She hadn't, so even the taste was all new to her. She devoured it and left a mess that took nearly an hour to clean. Neither Janet nor Logan cared about any of that. They cleaned it up without complaint and looked fondly on their little girl who had quite clearly enjoyed her day.

Only a short month after she turned one, she had taken her first steps. Logan had been lucky enough to be there to see them, and he would never forget them. She had not walked to mommy or daddy, or even to a familiar room. She had taken her first steps from the sofa in the direction of Phoebe, the little Tabby cat they had adopted from a woman outside a grocery store a few weeks prior. He and Janet had both laughed, and that cat became her best friend and closest confidante. She would walk to see that cat every chance she got.

When the time came for her first day of school, Logan had dropped her off and Janet cried in the passenger seat. He tried to console her but that wasn't going to happen. He didn't cry then, but there was a lump in his throat that whole day. He remembered carrying her to the car asleep because she was exhausted from all of the activity and excitement that had in the classroom. He buckled her in her seat and watched her sleep for a few minutes before driving home.

The first time she picked up and book and carried it over to him and sat on his lap to read it, she was six. She chose "Goodnight Moon" and he listened to every word even though he already knew the story because he had read it to her a million times. She missed a lot of the word pronunciations, but she tried so hard. She came to him almost every night and did the same thing. Before long, she was reading him chapters of novels. He loved when she sat on his lap and read to him. He would never forget it. Much like everything she did, he would never forget it.

Of course none of the things he recalled were true. He had never been there for any of those things. And all he could think about driving down the California highway was that he regretted missing so much of her life as she grew up. Janet had been there for all of it and described it in detail, but she had grown to despise Anisa over time. The only concrete memories he had were from after Janet and Anisa started constantly arguing and forcing a wedge between themselves. He missed so much of life with them that he hadn't seen them imploding and splitting from one another.

After two long hours of driving, he came up on the house he had left his daughter at thinking she would be safe long enough for him to find

Janet and bring them all back home safely. He despised just how wrong he had been about it all. He parked the rental car at the end of the driveway and walked to the door of the house. He hadn't even knocked when two sets of incredibly strong arms grabbed him and yanked him inside. On his left arm was Jaguar, and on his right was Grizzly. They threw him down on the sofa and stared at him as if he were a museum display they couldn't figure out.

"Ah, Logan Aster," came the voice he knew but hated more than any other now. "So glad you decided to join us."

"You didn't leave me much choice, Nestor! You threatened to kill my daughter if I didn't come."

"Oh, I guess I did, huh?" said Nestor with a huge grin. "Well, anyway, I am happy you came…and alone. I forgot to add that part to the note, so I am glad you read that into it."

"Been in this business a long fucking time. I know not to involve people in things like this."

"Good, good," he said. "So, why have I brought you here? Care to guess?"

"I have no clue, but I wasn't about to just sit back and let you kill my daughter because I didn't do anything."

"Hmm, let's have a little chat before we do anything else. I want you to think about why we are here, in this situation in the first place. Is it because of something I did?" asked Nestor.

"Yes, it's because you took my fucking wife, you asshole."

"Oh, I knew you would go there with it. Be honest for once. We are here because of what you did. Or rather didn't do. You were given an order and you refused to carry it out. There were consequences, and you are now in the middle of them."

"They were supposed to be for me, not for them. Do what you want with me. Leave them alone."

"I am afraid that's not an option. When I ordered you to kill them, it wasn't to be ignored. If you aren't going to do it, then someone has to.

Hell, I will give you one more opportunity to show your loyalty to Animal Kingdom. I have never done this before, but a second chance seems warranted since you were so new and perhaps didn't quite grasp the severity of your disloyalty."

"What? No! I am never going to kill my own child. That is never going to happen. I will gladly give myself up if you let her go, wherever she is."

"Ha ha, you are going insane a little at a time, aren't you? I know you heard me the first time. That isn't going to happen. What would it say about me if I let her go and let you take her punishment?"

"She isn't being punished, though. I am."

"In all fairness, you both are," said Nestor. "Okay, here is the deal. You didn't follow through on an order from a superior. That's bad. You ignored warnings about what would happen to you if you did, and you still failed to finish. When you became a target, you went after me and my men. I cannot count how many are dead now. I was shocked to learn that you gathered a team too. I thought you were a lone wolf, pardon the pun."

"I have a team because I knew I couldn't do it alone. I am not stupid. I know when I am overmatched."

"But…you are overmatched now and here you sit in a room with me and two other men alone. Unless you are trying to tell me you aren't actually alone and I need to be wary of what's coming."

"I am alone, that much I can tell you. I thought you would be alone too, that's why I came without a backup plan."

"That was fucking stupid on your part. Why the fuck would I be by myself and call on the most dangerous man I know to come meet with me when he is aware I have his child and have threatened her life? I would have to be as stupid as you are for trusting me and coming here at all."

Logan did not like the sounds of that. He hadn't noticed that Jaguar had left the room. He had been far too enamored with what Nestor was saying. He stared hard at the man, wishing for a chance to rip out his throat or snap his neck.

"Daddy? Is that you?" asked Anisa from a place in the room to his right. He looked around frantically and then laid eyes on her. She had both ears and earrings. The package had been part of a horrible game, a ruse to get him here and nothing more. He saw also that she had all her fingers. He didn't know how he could have been so blind. He thought back to the moment he had opened the packages and couldn't see anything in his mind's eye that told him they didn't belong to his child. He would look again if he got a chance.

A chair had been placed in the center of the room, directly in front of Logan but too far away for him to reach. Anisa was tied to the chair by her wrists and ankles and then Jaguar sat back down next to Logan. Nestor walked up to Logan and put his face in Logan's face. He smelled of cigar smoke and whisky. He got close enough that the hair of his face scratched Logan's skin. "I want you to remember that this is all because you would not do what was asked of you. Your failure to show more loyalty to our organization than to your family."

"You don't have to do this, Nestor. You can still walk away from this with your life. If you do this, I guarantee you that you die."

"I don't care about living or dying. I care about justice and doing what needs to be done. If I let you off, then all of the others I have punished seem like a waste. They will all be angry with me for not giving them their second or third chances. I am not going to be that person."

"I am warning you, motherfucker! You do this, there is no coming back from it."

"I have been over that line for a lot of years, Logan. I was never hoping to come back from anything. All I wanted was to show you how deadly serious loyalty is to me and my organization. The men holding your arms each had to do something similar, and they did it with no complaints. Now, they are the best at what they do and they make a lot of money for me."

"If you are over that line, I beg you not to go further. Even if you can't get back, you can keep my respect and your dignity. You don't have to do it."

"What if I told you that I want to do it, Logan? How would that make you feel? If I said I thought you deserve it? I know you want to kill me and I am not going to make it easy for you, but I am going to give you a hell of reason to want it." He stood up and walked to Anisa in the chair. He stroked her hair and she withdrew. She couldn't go anywhere, so he smiled and continued. He placed his hands on her shoulders as he walked behind the chair.

Logan was sweating and becoming shaky. He knew what was coming and he thought about a billion ways at once to stop it but none of them were feasible. He didn't want to cry, but he was beginning to feel tears in his eyes. They dripped slowly out and rolled down his cheek. He looked into the face of his teenage daughter and she was crying silent tears as well. Logan noticed the recognition in her face. She knew what was happening and she was terrified. When Logan didn't jump to his feet or run for her, she knew she was beyond assistance.

Nestor had withdrawn his pistol from a holster on his leg and was caressing it. He looked hard at Logan who was doing everything he could not break down. Nestor placed the barrel of the gun at the back of Anisa's head. He looked down at the floor for a brief second, steeling himself for what he was about to do.

Logan tried to stand, but the two sets of strong arms grabbed him and restrained him. Anisa looked at her father as he struggled and then she screamed.

"Daddy, help me!"

The gun sounded like a bomb in the small space and the bullet destroyed the bone and flesh of Anisa's head. The jet of blood through the front sprayed Logan, Jaguar, and Grizzly. Her head slumped and her eyes were wide open, the terror still present in them. The blood fell from her wound like milk pouring from a spilled glass. "Consequences," said Nestor.

"I will fucking kill you, motherfucker!" screamed Logan, who still could not move due to the arms holding him tightly to the spot.

"No, you won't. At least not today." He turned and walked out of the room, uttering one last thing before completely disappeared from view. You know what to do with him."

Right on cue, Blue and Pink came through the door with rifles aimed at the men holding Logan. They hadn't known beforehand what they were in for, but Logan had told them to expect guards. If he was guessing, he would have said five or six, so two was really painting a positive picture for his help.

"Don't fucking move!" said Blue to both men on the sofa. "Let him go and stand up slowly."

Both men complied since they didn't have weapons of their own. They stood and looked at one another. They had no options and attacking the two people with rifles was the best and quickest way to a grave that they could see. It was only smart for them to do what they were told just in case. As Blue and Pink bound them, Torrance came in the door as well. He took one look at Anisa and shook his head in absolute disgust.

"Walk," said Blue as he guided them to the vehicle waiting outside. "Try anything and I take off your heads…both of you for the price of one fuck-around."

"What are you doing here?" Logan asked Torrance.

"I didn't want to miss it if there was any excitement." He looked mournfully at the body of the girl in the chair. "Is that her, Aster?"

"Yes, that's my baby, Anisa. He shot in the head right in front of me. I have no idea where he went but we are taking those henchmen of his with us and getting answers."

"I think now I will let you have the kill shot, Aster. I don't know what I would do if someone killed someone I love that way. Of course, I don't love anyone, but I did when I was younger."

"No kids then? Ever?" asked Logan, looking away from the body.

"Oh, I had two children," said Torrance. "I said I didn't love anyone. I mean, I took care of the kids, but love wasn't an emotion I was too fond of."

"I never thought I would have, much less love, a child. I loved her more than life itself. I would have given my life for hers in a second but that fucker refused to let me the martyr I was trying to be."

"We will get him. You have my word."

"Oh, I am going to get him, help or no help. I am going to hunt his ass down and dismember him with a butter knife."

"Careful. Don't be too cocky. He isn't gonna let you walk in and walk all over him. He has shown he is formidable. You will need a plan and you will need to be prepared for anything."

The four of them drove back to the airport with the hostages in the trunk of the rental car. They could not fly commercially with hostages, so they chartered a plane where no questions would be asked. The man who flew them was an acquaintance of an acquaintance of Torrance and his businesses. It was a quick flight with no stops along the way. Once in Washington, DC, they landed at a private airfield and hailed a cab. It took them back to the house and they tied the men up in the basement, debating what to do with them. Logan knew they were going to be a bigger challenge than Greyhound when it came to answers, so he was going to need to step up his game significantly.

He was disappointed when the men offered to talk in exchange for their lives. They didn't want to be tortured and risk dying, so they pleaded and begged until Logan agreed that their cooperation would grant them their lives…for the time being. He made clear that if they engaged them at any time after being released, they would become fair game. Both men agreed to the terms and spilled information like a singing canary. Logan wanted to know where Nestor had gone and who or what was protecting him. The men spoke of what they called Hulk Fortress.

"What the fuck is Hulk Fortress?" asked Logan. "I want details."

They described a compound that resembled a massive prison. It was made of concrete like everything else the Animal Kingdom built or bought. The part standing above ground was a façade. There was no one in that section since the rest of it was burrowed underground. Around the entirety of the building were guard towers that each contained three guards with automatic rifles and lots of training using them. Many of them were not part of the Kingdom but worked to pay off debts to Nestor or other high ranking members. In the guard towers there were ladders that retracted so getting up would be impossible. There was a total of eight towers around the property with two in each quadrant: north, south, east, and west. Logan's quick math told him that was 24 guards, and that was going to be tough enough without what was coming once they accessed the inside. Jaguar told them that once inside they would encounter roughly twenty to thirty men, all ready and willing to die to protect what was inside, both people and objects. He didn't elaborate, but Logan had an idea what he was referring to.

"What kind of firepower are we talking about?" asked Torrance, surprising Logan.

"A lot," said Grizzly. They are defending a fortress that no one is supposed to get into. There is a lot of stuff there people will die or kill for."

"A lot is a shitty answer. Do better," demanded Logan.

"The outer guards will have AK-47s and AR-15s. They will have more ammunition than they would ever use in a gunfight with four people. You are not going to cause them to run out and then ambush them. Drop that idea before it reaches your brain," said Jaguar.

"What about inside?" asked Torrance. "You can't leave that out and expect us to guess."

Grizzly cleared his throat. "They will have an array of assault rifles. If you can think of it, someone inside will have it. There is no designation of who gets what. They are all trained for use on more than a few weapons. If you get in there, you are gonna need protection."

"Where will we find Nestor when we get in there?" asked Blue.

"Who?" asked both men simultaneously. "We know him as Komodo," said Jaguar.

"Then answer the fucking question. Where will we find him once we get inside?" asked Logan.

"He has a bunker inside. Basement two. You will not be able to get in there. You have to wait for him to come to you," said Grizzly.

The more they talked, the more confident Logan and the others became that they had enough information to make a successful invasion of the fortress and that they could walk away having eliminated the organization and its leader. Logan was coming up with ideas in his mind as his captives spoke and before long, he had a complete picture in his head of how they would do it and he was reasonably confident that they would do it without losing anyone else.

As promised, when they had given all the information they had to offer, the two men were set free. They were blindfolded, driven to a new location and released like wild animals that had eaten the vegetation in an angry grandmother's garden. They climbed out of the car and went on their way, never looking back at the people who had taken them hostage and used them for answers that about their boss who was sure to be pissed and possibly kill them once he found out about their betrayal.

CHAPTER ELEVEN

They had finally been able to get the location of the fortress from Grizzly before letting him and Jaguar go, and they were unsurprised to learn that it was nearby. They had to go south again, but not too far. It was located in a small place in North Carolina called Stonebrook. It was neither located anywhere near a brook, nor was it remarkable in any way for stones of any kind. It was one of those city names that apparently came from nothing more than the imagination of a person in need of a name for a place by a certain time or for people who mattered.

Logan had done a little research on it over the past few hours and he was sure they could get there and put the plan in action within the next twenty-four to forty-eight hours. The only thing impeding them at the moment was a lack of weaponry that compared to that the hunters from Animal Kingdom had told them to expect once they got on the property. The only way to get what they needed was to go to a military surplus store, and even then, the weapons they were looking for weren't guaranteed to be accessible.

They checked all of them that they found on the way and picked up some items at each one. Before all was said and done, they had what they needed despite it taking a half dozen stops to accomplish it. Now, they were clean and clear to keep driving into North Carolina. They sped faster than the speed limit and never even saw a cop as they moved through the countryside. The views were stunning with everything from mountain and streams, to cliffs, farms, and beautiful houses fit for no less than millionaires.

When they got to the white, shiny sign with ocean-blue lettering telling them they had arrived to the city, it was already past noon. They needed to find a place to stop and recoup before they trekked out the following morning at 5:00 to take down the enemy, hopefully once and for all. The trunk was full of guns and explosives that they planned to use during the incursion, and they would stay there since bringing them into a hotel in the state of today's society was probably the biggest mistake any person could make. They would be lucky to make it as far as the desk before someone gunned them down. It would be embarrassing if their mission got fucked by a "good guy with a gun" because they were trying to bring guns into a place where they didn't belong.

The hotel they chose was called BrookVille and it was a shabby little thing with only twenty total rooms. There was only one level and they were placed in room 15. The room had two beds, so some sharing had to be done, but no one minded too much. It was only for one night. The worst that could happen would be sharing a bed with a person who made money killing, dealing drugs, selling weapons, or trafficking girls. It applied to all of them so who would really care?

They enjoyed the time and spent it thinking about things other than what was coming in the next phase. They slept peacefully and when they awoke with a call from the concierge at 4:00 in the morning, they got into go-mode fast. They dressed in armor under their regular clothing, and then they walked downstairs where they checked out and left. They got into the car after making sure all of the weapons were untouched, and then made for the fortress on the other side of town. From what Logan could find on the internet, it was a secluded and minimally inhabited location. There didn't seem to be any other buildings or anything around that would contain people who would be set on edge by the potential firefight.

When they got in view of the mammoth structure that acted as fortress for the Animal Kingdom, all of their eyes were wide open and focused on the enormity and difficulty of the task ahead of them. Logan parked the car a good distance away so they had to walk, and he anticipated there would be sensors at this place the same way there was at the place in Maryland. This could even have things that one didn't, such as lighting, cameras, exterior weapons, or guards that the captives had not mentioned for obvious reasons.

The walk was scary since they were strapped with guns and other dangerous devices. Had anyone seen them, it was likely they would have been reported and the whole thing could collapse before it even got started. They were facing the same risk of frightening people into shooting them here walking in public as they would have been if they carried the same weapons into the hotel.

The concrete monster stood on a hillside by itself surrounded by trees and a retaining wall that was five feet high. It was clearly designed to keep people out, and that was precisely what the team didn't need. The closer they drew to the destination, the more the challenge grew in Logan's mind. Perhaps they didn't know about the wall because it was new, or maybe they had been keeping stuff to themselves, but either way, there was a literal wall keeping them from completing their mission.

"We need to find a way over that wall without being seen," said Logan knowing full well that all of them were thinking the same thing. "Our other option is to take a long way and head around."

"There is no way over, I am willing to bet," said Torrance who had a compound of his own that he worked diligently at keeping people out of. "If this fucker is smart, and from what I have seen he sure as hell is, then he put that wall there for people to try and climb because there is an easy way in and the average person will not look for it. Think of it like the vulnerability on the Deathstar. It looks menacing so people treat it like it is and never expect a susceptible spot."

Logan looked at the man, glad they had brought him along. He was going to be more useful than Logan first thought, especially considering the keeping people at a distance was one of the things he prided himself on. Logan had begged to get inside and was still almost refused. Thinking back, there was absolutely no way that he could have gotten in on his own. Then the words he had just heard hit him. There must be such a spot in Torrance's camp that people failed to look for, the same way he had.

"How do we approach it then?" asked Blue. "All I see is wall all the way down and around?"

"I think we should split up, but keep our eyes on one another. We can take different areas and radio back if we find anything," said Pink.

"Good plan," said Logan. "We go our own ways and look for a way in."

"Let's do it," said Torrance.

The group split and went in all different directions: Logan and Torrance to the north directly for the wall, Blue to the east, Pink to the west. They searched for any sign of weakness and found nothing resembling one. They moved closer and that was when the radio sparked to life and the voice said something that they didn't expect. It could not be as simple as that, but why spend time arguing about it or doubting it?

"You aren't gonna fucking believe this!" said Torrance. "There is a door at the far end of the wall that we can easily pick."

"Son of a bitch! The easy way in," said Logan half to himself but saying it into the radio by accident at the same time.

They all navigated to the door Torrance spoke of and were shocked beyond words when it opened with the ease he had promised. It didn't prompt any alerts to sound and there weren't any sensors. It genuinely felt like Nestor did not expect anyone to find the door as it was hidden from the majority of the world since they wouldn't be experts in securing a vital campus.

Immediately on entering, they saw exactly what Jaguar and Grizzly had told them they would encounter. There were two towers on each corner of the structure, each of them twenty feet tall. In each of them they could see the three guards they were warned about. According to the plan they had mapped out, Logan and Pink crept to the farthest corners, opposite one another, and set up their rifles. They were supposed to take out six towers worth of guards and then Blue and Torrance would scale the others and take theirs out hand-to-hand. They didn't have the gun skills that Pink and Logan did, so it caused problems when it came to necessity of accurate shooting from a distance.

The first thing Logan did was apply the silencer so that the shots would not be heard by other guards and they could not trace it back to his location. As long as all of the guards believed they were under heavy fire, they would not anticipate an old man and a younger old man climbing up the wood leg of the tower to engage them in hand-to-hand combat. With his scope sighted and the silencer operational, Logan fired the first shot.

In the tower nearest to him, a guard fell flat and made a thud as he did so. The other guards in the tower with him looked around for the source but found nothing. One checked the wound and assumed the trajectory, and then immediately set his automatic rifle to fire spurts in that direction. Fortunately for Logan, he was off by a few feet so none of the shells hit him. He still had the advantage.

On the other side, Pink had prepared her weapon the same way, and as soon as Logan opened fire, she copied the move and took out her first guard as well. She was less patient than Logan so she fired in succession. She took down an entire tower in a matter of seconds. She moved not-so-subtly to the next tower, and that was when she was spotted. She tried to dive out of the line of fire, but the rapidity of the shots made it impossible. She took two shells to the chest and fell backward.

Logan didn't see what was happening until it was too late. One of the guards sounded the alarm and then all hell broke loose. The guards took up positions and shined lights on the team, seeing them all with no issues. They began firing rapidly at them all, and before long, there was only chaos. The team had not prepared for such an outcome and now they were improvising every move they made. Logan put his gun on automatic and took aim in the direction of the towers, not intentionally hitting anyone but attempting to draw fire away from the others.

Across the yard, Pink was getting back to her feet after enduring the two shots. Without the armor, she would be sporting two huge holes in her chest. She appeared to be okay, so Logan didn't make any effort to protect her. The action all around her prevented any of the soldiers or guards from seeing her and she took the opportunity to follow Logan's lead once again. She was firing on automatic when she started to hit guards and soldiers with consistency.

At the top of one of the towers, Logan could see that Blue was facing off with two guards that neither he nor Pink had eliminated. He didn't have time to watch the whole battle, but Blue was holding his own well. Logan turned his attention back to the firefight and wiped out more soldiers. Blue was finished with his one-man show and climbed back down to the ground, grabbed his weapon from the hiding place where he had stuck it, and then took to helping his teammates.

It was over sooner rather than later and all of the enemy combatants were down. Logan wasn't sure they were all dead, but it was sensible to believe they all were. With that part of the task complete, the team moved to the main entrance. They were more cautious than they would have been if the first part of the operation had gone smoothly. Now they had to assume people inside were hearing what was happening outside and taking measures to act appropriately if those outside made it inside. Logan kicked the door down with ease considering he still occasionally felt intense pain from the injury to his back in his time with the Marines.

No one entered at first, and it was a good decision since pistol fire was directed right at the door. Two people waited on each side of the frame, and when the man from inside with the gun stepped out, Logan grabbed his arm and twisted it behind his back, snapping his shoulder out of place and then Blue twisted his head, breaking his neck. No more shots emitted from the house so they all went in, still prepared for the worst.

The room was empty, except for a couple of soldiers who seemed to be busy with other things and paying no attention to the new intruders. Torrance took them out with two quick shots from a pistol before they even knew there was anyone in the room to shoot them. The team moved to the first room, and they found no one there. They repeated the process in every room. When it became clear that they were going to have to delve into the basements, they became wary. There wasn't a lot of space and they would not have any kind of advantage.

Hardening themselves, the four went to the basement door and descended the stairs. The room was larger than any they had ever been in and it was filled with soldiers holding guns. Just as Logan had most feared, they were walking into a war they couldn't win. The only thing that allowed Logan the courage to continue was the armor he was wearing to protect him from bullets.

Logan, who still had his rifle set to automatic, fired sporadically into the crowd, and they scattered fast, returning fire from their makeshift shelters. The constant fire was destroying the wood of the tables and chairs, ripping it to shreds. Following Logan as was the natural order, the other three also opened fire in the large room. Shards of every kind of material flew into the air like it had been caught in a windstorm. The sounds of the rapid fire were like a horrifying fireworks display that guaranteed death to its viewers. Muzzles flashed and created a freak and mesmerizing effect in the poorly-lit room.

All four had taken some kind of impact and lived to fight on. The armor doing its job insofar as no one had yet perished. Logan made a bold move and took off one of the grenades on his chest. He pulled the pin and tossed the explosive into the room with reckless abandon. Three second after tossing it, it exploded and the flash was bright enough to blind anyone not prepared for it. The intensity of the blast threw the team back several feet, but it didn't harm them. The only thing left in the room was the bodies of the men who had been unlucky enough to choose today to stand watch there. Logan and the others moved through the room and came to another door. This one was locked and there was no way to open it.

Torrance, an expert with picking locks, couldn't even get it to budge. They planted a small amount of C-4 and still nothing happened. It was like breaking into a safe but worse. Logan tried different tools and utensils but they got him no closer to entering that door. The fact became clear when they had tried everything they could: they needed to leave and come back and try again later. They had fired thousands of rounds and made more noise than a Mardi Gras parade, and still the people in basement two did not feel compelled to exit and see what was happening on the surface. It was going to take more than what they had already tried, and Logan hated the idea. He wanted it to be easy. He wanted to come here and walk away successful, but that wasn't going to happen this time.

Gathered outside once again, the team was on its way off the property when the most unexpected face appeared before them and the man it belonged to held a pistol in Logan's face. The man known only as Jaguar stood before him with a sinister look and what appeared to be glee at finding him here. "Nobody fucking move or I blow his fucking head off!" said Jaguar. Just as he finished speaking, the other one, Grizzly, appeared from nowhere and held his weapon aloft.

"You are all coming with us," said the beast of a man. "Follow us, or die right here."

They did as they were told, walking at a cautious pace as they were creeping ever closer to the house they had only just escaped. Logan was breathing heavily, anxiety and fear permeating his being. He was not afraid of dying or even going up against the man who had killed his little girl. His fear came from putting the others in dangers when he tried what he was thinking. He attempted to push the thought away, knowing it was risky for everyone, but the nagging nature of it convinced him it was the only chance they had.

With Jaguar walking behind him and Grizzly behind Blue, he did a quick drop and swept the foot of his guide and as he fell to the ground he wrapped his wrist and dislodged the gun, knocking it several feet away. Before the other guide had a chance to react, Logan got behind his back and pressed his knee firmly into the spine and pulled back on the shoulders, causing him to drop his gun as well. Torrance kicked the weapon away and then took out his own and put it to the temple of the man closest to him which happened to be Grizzly.

"Now, you don't fucking move!" said Torrance, angry and on the verge of ripping the man limb from limb.

"You are gonna stay right here, on your knees, until we are gone. If you so much as turn your head, I will kill you both…and I can do it from a long way away," said Logan. "Any questions?"

They both nodded their heads to suggest they knew exactly what was expected of them. They got on their knees and rested there while the four others ran away into the darkness that was quickly becoming daylight. Not wanting to make an appointment with a bullet to any part of their bodies, they didn't move a muscle. They didn't know when it would actually be safe to move again, so they waited for ten minutes before doing so. When they stood and there were no repercussions, they went inside and found the disaster that awaited them.

Logan and the others were far from safe, and Torrance let them know what he thought about how cooperative the men had been when they had the upper hand the whole time. It was right in front of their home and they could easily have made a call to have someone meet them and assist. The fact they didn't wasn't something that Torrance was taking lightly. "There is no way they let us go that easily without some kind of a plan," he said. "If nothing else, we are being monitored. My assumption is, we are being tailed."

"Who would be following us?" asked Pink. "We would have seen or heard someone if they were behind us."

"You misunderstand, Pink. I am not saying they came after us, I am saying they followed us. They could have cameras or spotters."

"So, they might know where we are, but if no one is physically here, then we can get away with relative ease," said Pink naively, forgetting the man she was speaking to was an expert in the same kinds of tactics he was describing.

"Your naiveté is charming. I wish I could still see the world so innocently. I am long past believing in the good of people," said Torrance.

"So, what do we do, boss?" asked Blue. "If they are watching, then there is nowhere we can go that they can't follow."

"There is one place," said Pink. "We can go back to the camp in Mexico. They can follow but they can't get in."

"No, terrible idea. They would know our most well-guarded secret: our location. I cannot risk that I don't expect you to either," said Torrance earnestly.

"Then where, Torrance? We cannot just sit here in the open waiting for them to come to us!" said Logan, growing frustrated at the lack of a plan, something they should have prioritized before trying to infiltrate the hideout of a mercenary and his soldiers.

"I say we lure them out, stay visible, and then lead them back here while we are in front and hunker down inside and use it as a base," suggested Blue as if it was going to be as simple as he was making it sound. He rolled his eyes at his own suggestion when he heard it out loud. It couldn't have sounded any more ridiculous.

"Okay, there is a place we can go. It is a base in Florida. It is not mine, but the man who owns the building owes me more than a few favors. He won't mind giving it up for a day or two."

"Then it's settled," said Logan. "We follow you to Florida and hope they follow. Does your 'friend' have men he can loan us? I am guessing they won't be sending their scrubs now that we took out a houseful of devoted soldiers."

"I will ask, but we aren't exactly close. I wouldn't call us friends, but maybe acquaintances or whatever is less than that."

"Make the fucking call. I don't have time for a life story. We need to get there sooner rather than later. This has to end."

"I'm on it," said Torrance. "Does anyone have a phone I can borrow? I don't carry on in the field. Cannot afford to be tracked by enemies."

Logan handed his phone to the old man who walked away to use it. He was nodding, which Logan took as a good sign, but then he touched something on the phone and his expression changed. It didn't look like such good news any longer. His face was pale and he hung his head. He was speaking slowly but not so much that Logan could read his lips.

After a few minutes, he came back over and handed the phone to Logan with a sweaty palm.

"What's wrong? Why do you look so pathetic?" asked Logan.

"Um, when I took the phone, there was a second call. It was the morgue in DC saying that Anna's body was there and needed to be claimed."

"It's Anisa, and her body is here?" asked Logan, not sure he had heard correctly.

"Yeah, here in the city morgue. I'm sorry Aster. I cannot imagine how you are feeling."

"I will deal with that soon. What about your call?" asked Logan, growing impatient.

"I spoke to him and he said the compound is ours along with his men. There are fifty there now, but he can provide more if we need it. We have to pay them, but that isn't a problem. I don't have men to pay any more since they are all dead but these two."

"Okay, so we head to Florida in two days. I need to deal with the Anisa situation first. I want to have a funeral and a goodbye for her. I don't care how any of you feel about it. I am not asking."

"You have my support," said Blue.

"Mine too," echoed Pink.

"While I think it is a stupid fucking idea, I understand why you want to do it and I am not about to try and stop you," said Torrance.

The group made two detours: one to the store to buy clothes that looked somewhat presentable and the other to the morgue to see and claim the body of Logan's daughter. He cried when he saw her and he didn't care who was looking. He caressed her hair and his tears dripped on her face and head. She looked beautiful having been made up to look like a new person. Now, more than ever, he had trouble restraining his rage and the desire to do things to the man who took Janet and now killed Anisa that had not yet been invented.

CHAPTER TWELVE

Nestor sat in his bunker, safe from atrocities occurring only a few feet from him and listened to the familiar sounds of chaos. He could have gone up and finally eliminated Logan once and for all, but he chose instead to leave it in the hands of his capable followers. He paid them enough that they could and should die for him if it came to that. He smiled at the idea of all of those men giving their lives not realizing he didn't care about them or what they brought to his organization, because the truth was that only five men in the organization mattered at all: him, Grizzly, Jaguar, Piranha, and Shark. They were the ones who hunted and did the dangerous stuff out in the real world. They weren't afraid to get their hands dirty and do what others were so hesitant to do. "What's the count?" he asked Piranha as he came back in the secure room from assessing the damage outside of it.

"It's a fucking mess, boss. All of the guards outside are dead and the soldiers inside, same thing. They left no one alive. I did find Jaguar and Grizzly out front though. Said Aster and his men ambushed them and let them go in exchange for their safe exit."

"Okay, good," said Nestor. "What about the monitor?" he asked Shark who was hard at work on the computer keeping track of the team as they fled.

"They are still in the area. Went to the hospital on Dunleavy, not sure why. They don't appear to be in any hurry to leave and they don't seem like they are planning to hide. I think they are expecting us…you…to do something."

"They are not going to be disappointed in that respect. We are going to do something. Gather whoever is left in Gregor, and bring them here. Wherever these motherfuckers go, we will be right there to hit them."

"I will call Gregor Place," said Grizzly who had walked in halfway through the rant. "I will tell them to be here as soon as possible."

"Good. Get on it. Shark, don't lose them. Piranha, collect weapons and gear from the dead. I will put our plane on standby just in case they decide not to stay local. They invited a war and that is exactly what they are about to get. They may see us coming, and they may expect us, but they will never be ready for the firepower we are bringing with us. When everyone finishes with their tasks, gather the MODULE and pack it in the plane.

+++

Logan and the others had decided to cremate the body so Logan could carry it with him and dump it at her favorite spot when it was all over. He used her ashes as motivation to do it right and survive in the end. If he failed to do that, then Anisa would never get the ending she deserved. Logan could not bear the thought of failure, and he found himself wishing Janet was there with him to help him through what had become the darkest and most difficult time of his entire life.

With the urn among his belongings now, Logan loaded up one of the jeeps and the group headed for the base in Florida. The compound, according to Torrance, overlooked the ocean, and had a massive wall enclosing it that was twelve feet high and encircled the entirety of the structure. Unlike the fortress used by Nestor, this one didn't have a door that would allow simple access to any and everyone who felt compelled to get inside. At the top of the wall were platforms where snipers posted and aimed down at the land that was on the approach to the wall. No one could, in the words of Torrance, get within fifty yards if those shooters did not want them to.

"How hard will it be to assemble the men and get them organized for an attack?" asked Logan.

"Nassau said they were told to be on the alert for our arrival and do what we said from start to finish. I assume that means it will be rather simple to get them into gear."

"Nassau? As in Nassau Gettleman?" asked Blue?

"Yeah," said Torrance simply. "He owes me…a lot."

"You have got to be kidding me," said Blue. "He used to work for you and took men with him when he left. He is the reason there are only five elites now. How in the fuck can you work with him?"

"First, that's my business and my problem to deal with. Second, remember that you are an employee and that if you ever speak to me like that again, it will be the last thing that you do. Is that clear?"

"Sorry, boss. I just cannot believe you would turn to him of all people. I honest to god thought that asshole was dead."

"So, we are working with someone who already betrayed you once? Does that seem like the best course of action?" asked Pink.

"Look, before anyone else says anything about him, I know you two are unhappy and probably confused. Let me be clear about something. A couple things actually. First, I don't need either of your permission to do a goddamn thing when it comes to my work. In addition to that, it is not as simple as me working with him. I don't operate that way. You two should know that better than anyone else."

"What are you trying to say?" asked Blue.

"I haven't and never will forgive him for his betrayal. Instead, when I need his help I remind him what he did, tell him there are consequences like I do for anyone who betrays me, and then tell him that if I don't get what I am asking for, then they will suffer those penalties."

"Are you literally saying," asked Pink, "that you told him that he would be killed if he didn't help us?"

"In simple terms, yes. I threatened to kill him if he didn't offer me his place and his men."

"Wow," said Logan from the driver's seat where he had been listening and driving. "Sounds like he is scared shitless of something."

"Mr. Aster," said Torrance with a hint of anger. "He is one of those people who know me and what I am capable of. He betrayed me knowing he would be killed for it eventually, and he will be. When his usefulness to me expires, so does he. I just have to string him along enough to make him feel safe so he continues to work for me no questions asked. When you did what you did, you were a fucking child who had no idea the ramifications of your actions. That's why I agreed to give you an opportunity to wipe the slate clean."

"What did you do, Aster?" asked Pink who was only almost a teenager when the organization had been through the most challenging era of its long existence.

"Well," said Logan tentatively. "I may or may not have killed a man who was a big," and he was cut off by Torrance.

"The biggest…you can't get away with it by saying he was one the biggest, or just a big financier. He was the premiere one."

"Fine, Pink. I killed the biggest financier of Diamond Cartel and it sent them into a tailspin. I didn't know what I was doing when I killed him. I was following an order."

"It's never been bad since I have been there," said Pink simply. "If it was ever like that, I am glad I missed it."

"You're damn lucky you missed it," said Blue. "For a long time, there was talk about shutting us down completely. It isn't like we had skills marketable in other areas."

"Yeah, it came up a few times," admitted Torrance. "The only reason we didn't was because we got lucky and found a new financier who actually had more to offer and made things better for us. To this day, his son is still keeping us afloat almost single-handedly."

After the conversation died down, they drove in silence for a significant portion of the trip. The road was nearly empty in the city but once they reached the highway, the traffic grew intense. As time passed, it became bumper to bumper and then stalled outside of Jacksonville. As they continued on, they found a break in the traffic and then an opening on a straightaway. Logan sped up, knowing that he was falling behind his self-appointed deadline.

He was hitting top speed when the car next to them with tinted windows and no markings slammed into the front of the vehicle. Logan lost control and the vehicle skid, fishtailed and then flipped over on its side, landing with the driver door pinned to the pavement. It slid along the roadway for several yards before stopping and Torrance, Pink, and Blue jumped out of the top where the passenger side doors were still accessible.

It didn't take long until shots were ringing out and coming at the jeep. They hit the hood and tires, but Logan was unharmed as he scrambled to climb out the top as the others had done. He was sore but not injured. When he made it out, he cowered behind the overturned vehicle and Pink bravely went for the guns in the back. She retrieved them and a couple small explosives and handed them out to the others. Each took a post and fired on the car. No one had exited from it and they were shooting from the comfort of the interior with the windows rolled down only enough to poke out a barrel.

Torrance and Blue took out the tires and Pink went for the engine and related parts. Logan took his aim for the gas tank and fired one shot at a time. Traffic was starting to back up while getting too close to the black car for anyone's safety. There was no way Logan or any of the others could fire on auto and keep the people in those vehicles safe. With so many in the way now, there was no option of backing up for any of them. It was traffic invading a war zone where they didn't belong.

Blue wasn't one to take life into consideration when it was acting as collateral damage and that was exactly how he saw every car on the road. If they were stupid enough to get close to a gunfight, then they deserved whatever happened to them. With that thought on loop in his mind, he ripped the pin from a grenade without anyone noticing and tossed it at the black car. He didn't warn anyone of the impending blast and when it went off, it was a surprise to Logan, Pink, and Torrance.

The impact of the explosion flipped several cars next to the black one as well as that one. A fire was sparked in the bottom of the chassis and it quickly spread to other areas. Before long the whole car was engulfed. When the occupants exited, Blue shot them one at a time with his rifle. Logan was too stunned to do anything. Torrance was irate but he was in no mind to reprimand his soldier. Pink had no authority to say anything about it, but it was clear that she was livid.

When the scene was safe again, the emergency workers found six bodies from the car and another ten from surrounding vehicles, many of them children and young teens. Logan was able to vacate the area without being tied to it, though they had stolen a car to do so. He and Blue had taken all of the weapons and ammo from the back of the jeep and loaded it into the awfully conveniently placed Mercedes CLS53. There was no one inside and it was left running, so they took it. Logan was confident it would be some time before the cops cared about a stolen car when a multitude of people were dead from a highway firefight.

They made their way past the chaos and into the smaller cities. They were nearly home free. The sirens were in the distance behind them and all that lay ahead of them was the open world that led to their final destination. When the city sign for the place they were headed finally came into view, the feelings about what was coming started to surface in all four of them. They braced themselves and then when the car stopped, they jumped out to execute their mission.

Nestor could not believe what had just happened. He was trailing the other cars at a distance of ten lengths as was his custom when he was out in the field. He was cruising along with his driver hitting high speeds and making excellent time when suddenly the traffic halted almost entirely. He wasn't sure what was happening but it was Florida so it wasn't that much of a surprise when cars appeared seemingly from nowhere. There were on-ramps and merge lanes everywhere so it was sensible that vehicles would show up that had not been there previously. For a brief second, Nestor had lost sight of the small black car and got concerned that it had gotten away from him and they were going to have to find them again. "Where is the black car, Harris?"

"Ahead of us, sir. It is caught in the traffic too. I can see it," said the driver. "I will keep my eye on it, don't worry."

"Alright, then."

It was seconds after that when the car went out of sight for a short time and then came back with damage to the front. Nestor didn't know what had happened, but he had a hell of a good idea. It was something he taught his drivers…or rather paid someone to teach his drivers. He hadn't driven in over a decade on his own. From his vantage point he only just saw the jeep flip over and land on its side. He didn't expect what came next, but he enjoyed it briefly when his men fired shots at the jeep and pinned the bastards down.

His elation went to horror as a grenade was thrown that exploded and destroyed the car and burned the occupants. The blast rocked the vehicle he was in, but it didn't cause any kind of damage. They made the error of climbing out and that was when someone he couldn't see gunned them down one-by-one. He screamed in fury. "What the fuck!"

"Sir, the car has been attacked," said Harris obviously.

"I can fucking see the fucking car was attacked you fatass! Can you get us out of here?" asked Nestor.

"No, sir. We are stuck in a jam now. We cannot move until everyone else moves!"

"Dammit!" screamed Nestor. "Get me the fuck out of here, now!"

Harris tried backing up, and despite ramming several cars and trucks along the route, he still kept going. The man in the seat behind him would gladly kill him if he failed so some damaged automobiles were the least of his worries. When he got them free from the tangle, he drove the wrong way down the highway, weaving through the stopped cars as if they were part of a game. He found a spot to change to a lane that was not blocked off and jumped in it. Seconds later, they were once again able to pursue the assholes who had killed more of his men. The only problem now was they didn't have a clue what they were pursuing. The jeep was still overturned on the side of the road, so clearly they hadn't used that.

He had his answer not long after he thought about the question. A man was running up and down the road screaming about his car being stolen. He was wearing a black silk suit and silk tie. Without talking to the man, he knew the car was either brand new, expensive, or both. He got as far as he could go in one lane and moved the one Nestor was in, moving slowly past the wreckage. When he knocked on Harris' door, the big man rolled down the window and tried his best not to intimidate the smaller businessman. "Yeah," he said in his rough, gravelly voice.

"Excuse me," said the man. "I was wondering if you had seen anyone near a black Mercedes a few minutes ago. Someone has stolen mine and I didn't see anyone."

"I saw who did it," said Nestor from the back. "There were four of them. Three guys and a girl. They packed it with weapons and took off."

"What? Why would someone want to steal my car?"

"The same people who was in the jeep, I suppose."

"They stole my car because they cannot drive?" asked the businessman.

"Looks that way. We are heading that direction now. Sorry for your loss, but I really need to get going. I have an appointment I need to be at."

"Well, thanks for your help."

"Sure, whatever," said Nestor and then Harris pushed the man gently back and rolled the window back up. The car proceeded forward, now able to pick up speed. There was sure to be more than a few Mercedes cars on the road, but only one of them was stolen and full of weapons and dangerous people. They wouldn't want to be pulled over so they would go slow, and they wouldn't want to draw attention to themselves so they would play music and talk to one another like they were on a road trip. Nestor rolled his eyes thinking about the fake image they were probably presenting inside that stolen beauty.

+++

Logan was panicking after they were attacked. He was certain now that they had been followed, but he had no idea who was following them. It could have been the low-levels keeping tabs or it could have been the hunters coming to finish the job. Either way, he was worried that they had already begun to run out of time. The faster he drove, the more confident he grew about getting there and establishing a battle plan before the enemy arrived.

"What the fuck was that all about?" asked Torrance. He was glaring at Blue who knew he had really messed up and nearly killed them by trying to play badass hero with a grenade.

"They definitely followed us," said Logan. "They are probably on our tail right now, and if they aren't, then they will be soon."

"So, what's the plan?" asked Torrance. "Do we just get there and fly by the ass of our jeans?"

"No, no fucking way! We beat them there and set up a zone. We give everyone a job to do and place to do it from."

"There is no way we get there that far ahead of them," said Blue. "They were already right on our asses, so how do we create enough of a gap between us and them to give ourselves time for setting up something so elaborate?"

"We can hold out hope the traffic slows them down, but if it doesn't then we will have to reply on the head start and the speed. As long as we don't see a vehicle behind us showing signs of pursuit, then I think we are in the clear."

"What do we do if they arrive too soon?" asked Pink, bothered by the turn things had suddenly taken.

"If it comes down to that, then we wing it. We take them out before they take us out, by whatever means necessary."

By now they were within fifty miles of the destination and Logan realized no one was on the road in front of or behind them. He took the opening and pressed the accelerator as hard as he could and the sleek vehicle lurched forward, hitting top speed within seconds. There was little to no fear about being spotted or pulled over by cops this far from anything, so Logan kept the gas depressed for as long as he could until coming up on a few scattered vehicles on the road. He had to slow down anyway since he was within eyesight of the exit he needed.

He took the exit ramp and then they were only ten miles away. The anxiety was building. All of them felt the pressure of what was coming. They still didn't see anyone coming up on them, and they took that as a great sign. When they finally came up on the humongous property, their eyes lit up and they could hardly believe what they were looking at. It was in the middle of nowhere and looked like a prison for monsters. There was no way a human could get in or out without permission, but even inhuman creatures with powers would have difficulty.

The twelve foot wall did indeed encircle the house. Just above the top of the wall, the second and third floor of the house itself could be seen. The house was white and losing a lot of its color so there were spots on it that were blackened and covered in vines. The windows were dirty, but they were thick panes of glass that would not easily be penetrated by small-caliber bullets. The air was thick with the smell of pine trees and fish from a nearby lake. The stench was enough to make Logan want to plug his nose.

He pulled up to the gate that stood between the concrete sections of the wall and waited for a reply from the screen-microphone combo that was installed there. He was growing impatient when the thing finally beeped and an image appeared of a young kid with a crooked smile. "How can I help you?" he asked dutifully.

"Nassau sent us," said Torrance rudely. "Open the fucking door, now!"

"Oh, yes, Nassau did say we were expecting some people. Come on in."

"Stupid so of a bitch didn't even make sure we were the right people," said Blue. "I am guessing he doesn't last at that job for too long."

"No, definitely a high turnover rate at a job where you decide who is safe and unsafe to see the boss," said Torrance smartly. "My guards know to ask me and let me decide for myself."

Alright, we are here. Get the gear and weapons out and I will call the men to order," said Logan.

"Sure," said Blue.

"You got it," said Pink.

"Yeah, sure thing," said Torrance.

They worked together to unload the gear from the trunk of the car and carried it all into the large front room where it was thrown unceremoniously onto the floor. Logan had used a PA that the kid from the screen had shown him to call all of the people into the house into a meeting in the front room that was large enough to house a small city's populace. When they were all there standing or seated as they desired, Logan kicked the meeting into session and spoke quickly for fear they would be interrupted sooner rather than later. "Thanks for coming. I don't think we have much time, so I will lay this out there plainly and quickly." Everyone nodded assent without really knowing what was going on. "The four of us are here to basically adopt you to our little team and fight off a proverbial army that is on its way here. Each of you will have a task, and you will do it to the best of your ability or people will die. Who are the snipers?" Ten men raised their hands. "You know your responsibilities. You shoot anything that moves and doesn't belong here. The rest of you, Blue will give you assignments. Follow them to the letter. People are going to die today, but let's fucking make sure it is not our people."

All of the excitement and nodding died down as fast as it came. They were not looking forward to what this man had just introduced them to. They had been enjoying their day before the intrusion that was upending not just their afternoon but also their potentially their lives. Logan left to go take his position, and Pink did the same. They would once again be fighting opposite one another completing the same chore of mowing down the enemy.

With everyone in place, their jobs known and the plan to carry them out effectively playing like a video in their minds, Logan was prepared for whatever came for them. He assumed it would be different from the house in North Carolina, but there was no guarantee with Nestor. He had proven to be quite unpredictable. With weapons in hand, eyes on the distance, and minds in the right place, the new team was prepared for all-out war.

+++

The hunters were in a car behind the one Nestor was in. They never rode together, and it was a good thing. Nestor was so angry now that he was just short of being out of control. The Mercedes had never appeared and now they didn't know where it was and it was going to take extra effort and time for Shark to track them using the software that he employed. He had linked to a device each of them was holding or wearing, and since they were all undoubtedly together, finding one of them meant locating them all. While he worked, he kept Nestor up to date on the progress, which was too little at the moment for his liking. "Find them goddammit! How can we have lost them? We are on the same fucking road!"

"Working on it, boss. They are close, but the signal is kind of weak here. We are gonna have to get closer before I get a signal that really tells us anything we can use," said Shark. He was the tech genius of the crew but even he couldn't work magic when there was none to work. He hated being relied on for things that were near impossible. Among those things was tracking people without a method of keeping tabs on them. When the signal grew as faint as it presently was, then he was completely unable to use his skills with a computer or any other technological device for that matter. He kept trying.

"Fine, but let me know when we are close enough for a good signal. I wanna know where they are like yesterday."

151

"You got it, boss. I will let you know." Shark rolled his eyes. He didn't want to be at the beck and call of his boss when there was nothing he could offer him. It wasn't like the signal would become strong and he would keep the information to himself. He looked at the buses behind their car and shook his head. There was a day when he too had ridden back there, and it had been much different and even better at times.

The two buses bringing up the rear of the cavalcade were full of lower-level grunts who didn't have any idea where they were going, they were only following orders. They had been selected for their willingness to go into a combat scenario without any questions. They were prepared to give their lives for a cause that wasn't completely known to them. They were going in blind and may never walk out again, and they hardly flinched when Nestor told them what was at risk.

The drive was becoming tiresome for everyone, but suddenly there was a beeping on the monitor of the computer next to Shark and he perked up. Flashing on the screen was a symbol telling him the signal was at three-quarters strength which was more than enough for him to track the devices. He typed in some information and then he had a location, and to his elation it was closer than he had considered it might be. "Boss, I have a location. You are not gonna believe how close they are to here."

"Tell me," came the blunt reply.

"Five miles out. They are at a seaside resort or something. The place is huge. The devices are scanning the land and the object I assume is a hotel or house is massive. They seem to have taken to hiding after all."

"Hmm, that doesn't sound like something an assassin would do. If anything, they have found help. Perhaps the hotel is a hideout for a gang or something."

"Maybe," said Shark. "I guess we will find out in about twenty minutes."

Twenty minutes went by and then they were staring at the thing they had been so wrong about. Sitting the length of two football fields away was a mammoth house, if it could be called that, and around it was nothing. Nestor used his instincts to tell himself that this was not a regular house but they had come here for a strategic reason. He wasn't sure what it was, but the ideas formed in his mind faster than he could actually feel them out. They all climbed out of the vehicles except for those on the buses. "Shark, can you see how many people are behind that wall?"

"Not a fucking chance, boss. I have to get access to a camera for that, and all of the devices with cameras I am linked to show a black screen so they are either in a pocket or face down somewhere."

"Are you thinking they are not alone?" asked Grizzly. "This seems like the kind of place you would come if you wanted help."

"I don't think they are alone, no, but I don't know who or what is helping them."

"We have the power to storm in there and take them out, no matter what it is back there," said Piranha.

"I know we do, but we cannot be too hasty. If they have a plan in place, then walking in might be exactly what they want us to do," said Nestor.

"So, what the fuck do we do?" asked Jaguar. "We can't just sit here and talk about it."

"No, we aren't gonna sit here and discuss it," said Nestor. "We are gonna send them a fucking message they will not forget."

Pulling out an RPG like the one they had used against the invaders once already, Nestor positioned it on his shoulder and steadied it. Despite being such a great distance away, he was certain it would work the way it was supposed to. He aimed with the eyepiece and then slowly pulled the trigger that was tighter than that of a smaller gun. As he depressed it, he could feel the power in his hands and he loved the way it made him feel. He was confident that as soon as the rocket left the barrel, he would have them off guard enough to storm in and have him way with who or whatever was behind that wall. It went all the way and the smoke emitted from the back as the warhead jumped from the device and raced toward its impact point. He waited for it to make its collision with the concrete barrier and then for the detonation that would follow.

+++

All of the men from the house were at their posts and Logan and Pink were situated at the top of the wall with the snipers while Blue and Torrance were guarding the gate at the bottom. They had only just gotten settled when the cars parked a few hundred yards away in the distance. It was impossible for Logan to make out the types of cars or any kinds of details, but what he did see was six people climb out of them and start doing what he could only describe as socializing in the middle of the street. There were no other houses or people around so they were not obstructing anything, but it was odd to say the least. Simply out of curiosity and because no one else saw what he did, he looked through the scope of the rifle and sighted in the scene he was trying to decipher with his naked eye. As he got a clear picture, two buses pulled to a stop behind the cars and men, though no one exited.

Looking at the clear image, he saw that one of the men was indeed Nestor, and he could identify the others he knew as Jaguar and Grizzly from the other compound where they had encountered one another in less-than-ideal circumstances after taking the same two men hostage to get information from them. He wanted to shoot them then and there, but something told him not to draw attention to the house or himself. Try as he might, he could not make out any of the words they were saying since his lip-reading skill was amateur at best. The five hunters as they were known, climbed back into their car and Nestor grabbed something from the trunk of his. Logan immediately recognized it as an RPG and knew what was coming. "RPG, get the fuck down!" he screamed at the top of his lungs. "Off the wall! Go!"

Like rats in a tunnel, the snipers scurried to climb off of their perches and run to the more secure area on the ground. Of the twelve who were up there, all of them made it the bottom except for one. He was still on

154

the ladder when the wall exploded into a mess of concrete and metal from the rebar inside. The shrapnel spread in all directions with chunks of the wall hitting people and knocking them to the ground. It lasted for what seemed like forever, but in reality was only a few seconds. The hole left in the wall was mostly in the center so there was still room for five brave snipers on the platforms. Logan and Pink would undoubtedly be two of them, but when he made a call for three more, they all volunteered and decided among themselves who would do the deed. After making their choices, three men climbed up and took their positions again.

On the ground, people with medical training or simple concern for their fellow warriors were checking on the injured. Luckily, no one had been killed, but there was reason to believe that would change. Many of the wounded were severe and close to death. If they didn't get proper attention, then their demise was all but guaranteed.

Back up on the platform, Logan had once again taken aim, but what he saw this time was more terrifying than a rocket coming to obliterate his secure wall. The two buses were speeding forward, careening toward the wall with the intent of ramming it and bringing it the rest of the way down.

CHAPTER THIRTEEN

On Nestor's orders, the drivers of the buses were running at the wall at excessive speeds with the sole goal of hitting the barrier and bringing it crashing down. An added bonus would be taking the lives of the people on it or concealed behind it. As they drew closer, it became increasingly apparent that there was going to be serious damage to the vehicles as a result of the collisions, but Nestor was ostensibly willing to take such a risk since it was not actually him who was chancing anything. If everyone on each bus perished, he could always find more. It might hamper his immediate efforts, but once he retooled and came back, it would be like nothing was ever lost.

The first bus crashed into the wall on the driver's left. The front end bent like it was paper but the interior was undamaged. The other bus hit on the driver's right, and the same result occurred both inside and out. Each portion of the wall came collapsing down and when the dust cleared, there was nothing left of a wall to speak of. There were people running back and forth, trying to get to safety. Bodies lay strewn from one end of the yard to the other, blood and other gore dispersing into one massive, connected pool.

The buses both shot off steam like a volcano, and a fire ignited in one engine. The soldiers disembarked and, with weapons at the ready, charged into the waiting mass of enemy soldiers. Gunfire erupted from both parties and before long, they were engaged in a genuine battle, reminiscent of something from the Civil War more than modern times. Each bullet that struck a solder of Logan Aster was a small victory for Nestor Jacobson who was still watching from a remote location.

When the battle kicked into full go-mode, the hunters, armed with weapons and armor, something not afforded to the first wave of fighters, made their way to the house. After all the waiting and watching, they were finally getting their time to shine doing what they did best. Jaguar was the first on the property and he used a high-caliber pistol and shot head after head without breaking stride. All around him, people from both sides of the fight were falling. Next on scene was Piranha who used a katana and slashed his way past anything in his path. After him arrived Grizzly who withdrew his knives and went to work much the same way as his partner. Afterward was Shark, who in addition to being a tech genius, was a master with smaller caliber weapons. He used a pistol and downed many of the soldiers standing in his way. Finally, Komodo approached in all his glory. He looked much different dressed head to toe in armor and carrying an array of weapons. He strode up to the house with purpose, allowing the hunters to clear his route as he walked. He was in no danger since they would all four have to die before anyone so much as got a speck of dirt on him. He took the rifle from the sheath on his back and walked into the front room of the house, his target already sighted.

+++

From the moment the buses collided with the wall, all hell had begun to break loose. The falling wall had killed several people, and then the raging soldiers had taken out their fair share as well. At Logan's command, the others attempted to retreat back inside, but the appearance of the hunters ended that goal for several before they ever got a chance. Logan watched as one of them used a pistol of a high caliber, another a low caliber, one used a katana as easily as some people write with a pencil and the other used knives with the same ease. It was only when he saw Nestor that he understood what the objective was from the other side. It was to be an extermination.

The bullets flew and the bodies dropped, but that was only part of the plan. Logan and his initial team hid in the house to get positions. He watched as his men were slaughtered and it was only him, Blue, Pink, Torrance, and five soldiers left. The soldiers didn't hide and were dispatched rather quickly. Logan would see that many of Nestor's men were done for, but there were still plenty that could pose a problem for them before the hunters ever had to do anything. They charged on cue and Logan and his team went to work.

157

The first was easy, but as they kept coming, the challenge grew. Logan was engaged with two soldiers while Blue was fighting three of his own. Torrance was in a fistfight with one and Pink was being pulled by the hair by another. Logan didn't know what to do, so he did the simple thing and fought them with his hands. It was easier than he imagined since the men were more trained in weapons than anything else.

He stepped into his weight and took the first blow to his ribs in stride. It hurt but not enough to slow him. The next one came to his jaw, something becoming far too common. He stumbled but he didn't fall. He drew back his own fist and landed a blow to one of their noses, busting it open like a grape. It poured blood on him and the ground around them. He then placed a perfect kick to the man's gut and sent him flying a couple feet before he landed with a thud on the floor. He felt the pressure in his lower back where one of the men put the bottom of his foot. He caught himself before falling too far forward but the pain was too much to ignore. When he tried to swing his fist, he couldn't do it. The blow had weakened him far too much.

He couldn't continue the fight, but he had to. He took a pistol from his holster that he had previously emptied and used it as a club, hitting with the only strength he could muster. Despite being weak, the gun worked well to subdue the attack. With each strike he was able to weaken the opponent. When they were weak enough, he could strike the way he did it best. Each one met their ends after several strikes with a club when he reached over and quickly snapped their necks. It was a short reprieve before others went on the attack. He had to fight them the same way, and he did so successfully.

Pink had finally gotten her hair free of the clutches of the asshole pulling her around by it and was currently giving him an ass beating he would forget only when she killed him at the end of it. She had him pinned to the ground with her left knee with a blade to his throat using her left hand. She was pummeling his face with her right fist, each one bringing him closer to unconsciousness. After many blows, he lost consciousness and she walked away. She let him live, something that was not the norm in the middle of a typical war. She rectified her mistake as soon as he came aware and grabbed her leg. She knelt over, kicked the hand away, and planted the knife into his chest all the way to its hilt.

Blue was ending his fight on a high note as he slit through the throats of three men with the small blade he kept in his sock and pulled out only when it was called for. When a big man had him in a sleeper hold and he was losing his air, he thought it was in fact time, and he took the situation into his own hands. He was covered in blood from the exercise of slicing necks, but he was alive because of his quick thinking.

Torrance was able to easily and absurdly quickly for a man his age, dispatch his fighter. He made a spin move an NFL running back would be jealous of, got behind his man, gripped his throat tightly, and then jerked his hands in two different directions, snapping the neck with an audible cracking sound that could be heard over the ruckus. The man fell at his feet and he moved away like nothing had happened.

As if they were waiting outside for this exact moment, a second wave of fighters entered the room, but this one was better trained and harder to fend off, much like the levels of a video game would be as a player progressed through them. Logan knew they were still not fighting the main boss, so to speak, but the henchman that always preceded him in a game were tough as nails and took more hits and energy to get past. With that thought in mind, Logan bull-rushed his next opponent and was thrown to the side like an unwanted doll in the room of an angry child.

On cue, the others, a total of nine, came at Blue, Pink, and Torrance. Logan climbed back to his feet, shaking his head to clear the cobwebs. He was shocked that the man was armored and so damn strong. He jumped on the man's back who had thrown him and wrestled him to the ground. He rolled off and then as the man turned over, he rolled back and lodged an elbow in his chest, hitting the hard armor and doing no damage. It was going to take a lot more than that to conquer this group.

He rose to his full height and kicked him in the face. The one place they should have protected was their lone flaw.

The man's head flopped to the side and he was out like a light. Logan stripped a knife from the man's waist sheath and stabbed him in the chest, leaving him dead on the spot. Logan went to help his teammates as they were also struggling with their counterparts. Pink was losing her fight badly against three soldiers who had taken her by surprise. One of them was holding her arms behind her back and the other was punching her in the face while the third was stabbing her fruitlessly in the stomach where she wore thick armor.

Logan rushed to her aid and broke the hold of the man on her arms and slammed him to the ground. He reared back to drive his closed fist into his face when he hit a button somewhere and facemask deployed, covering the entirety of his face. Logan's fist landed on the hard glass and it reverberated throughout his whole arm. He was then forcefully pushed back and landed on his ass hard. He hadn't even got his bearings before he was socked on the right side of the face and then the left. He fell backward and the man was on him like a vulture on a corpse. He was attacking so fast and furiously that Logan didn't have a chance to react. He did the only thing he could at that moment and threw the man forward where his head slammed into the wall. It didn't hurt him but it dazed him just enough for Logan to rip off the helmet and batter his face with his fists. When he went lifeless, Logan found a new target.

Pink took the advantage Logan handed her and got the upper hand on both attackers, breaking the wrist of one and then dislocating the knee of the other with a swift kick that pushed it in the wrong direction to the point that it nearly broke off. Logan was matched with the one-wrist attacker now and he was easy prey. Fighting an elite fighter like Logan with one arm was not a good idea, and just to make it fitting, Logan broke his other wrist and forced him into a battle with his legs. With each kick, Logan deflected it and pushed it away. He took the butt of his gun and smashed the visor on his helmet, sending shards of glass into his face. He fell to the floor holding his hands over the place his visor once was and collecting the pool of blood that was dripping into them. Logan pushed him with his leg, hard, and he toppled.

Blue was fending off three feisty warriors who were slashing at him with blades. They were able, luckily, to only hit the armor he was wearing, but it was enough to keep him off balance. He threw an elbow into the throat of the one grabbing for his neck, and he flailed away temporarily. When he came back and was able to lock his arms, he kicked the one in front of him in the stomach and then used his weight to push back. He fell, landing on the man, and then stood to absorb the blow from the one he had kicked. He took the kick to his ribs and felt every bit of it in spite of the armor. He grabbed for it to soothe it and then was met with another kick, this one to the gut. He doubled over and took an uppercut to the chin that laid him out on his back. He rolled over and pushed himself to his feet, but at the halfway point was foiled by an arm around his neck and then weight forcing him to the ground. The man was on his back, strangling him and the two others were taking turns making mincemeat of his face. With every blow, he spit out more blood and felt less aware. Torrance ran to his rescue, shooting all of them in the back where the armor was weak.

Torrance attracted the attention of the final three and it did not look good for him as they swarmed him! He went beneath them like a victim in a zombie movie. They buried him but instead of biting him, they were pummeling him with their fists and kicking him with their steel-toe-booted feet. He could be heard making sounds of discomfort and even agony under the pile of bodies, and they had already landed a significant number of crushing blows before anyone could reach his to assist.

Blue was the first to get there and he tossed one man aside and then leapt on him like a cheetah on a zebra in the African plains. Pink lowered herself in a way she normally wouldn't and punched one in the balls so hard that he fell over holding them. She too pounced like a lion and went to work. That left one for Torrance and Logan to deal with, but Torrance was in no condition to go on the offensive. He lay battered, beaten, and bloody on the floor. Logan took it upon himself to settle the score with the man.

With Blue beating the shit out of one and Pink being most unladylike with the other, Logan made quick work of his quarry by punching him repeatedly in the face and head. He had removed the man's helmet so the shots would have more impact, and he hit him as if stopping was the wrong thing to do. With every swing of his fist to the head or face, he felt a renewed sense of energy. He understood that as soon as this group was eliminated, the real and final test for them waited just outside the door. He didn't want to go head-to-head with the elite killers known as the hunters, but the only other option was running, and that was something that not only did he not want to do, but frankly he was also sick of doing. In the last week he had run and hidden more than at any other moments of his life combined, and it was starting to wear on him.

One final shot to the face and his man went out cold. He dropped him to the floor in a heap and relaxed as Blue and Pink were finishing their fights as well. It was ridiculous how much like a bad movie the scene looked like, but they all knew that the situation and the danger was very real. They had come close on multiple occasions to dying in the last several minutes that felt like actual eternity, and it was only going to get worse with what waited for them next. That idea of a video game popped into Logan's head again, and he saw this level as the henchmen before the big bad boss. He was wrong thinking the other group bore that distinction. It was obvious now that as tough as they had been, they were still less of a challenge than the hunters. The hunters were trained with weapons and in hand-to-hand combat in a way that no one else was. They could take out armies on their own, and legend had it they had done exactly that on more than one occasion. If the rumors about them were put into writing, it would be an encyclopedia rather than a book. A single page would do to list the accomplishments Logan had in his career in comparison, and it was inarguable that he had done more than most people. Nestor didn't hire weaklings for that position, and the men on the other side of the door to the house were far from that. The respite was over as soon as they entered, ready for a conflict they were determined to end.

Nestor came in first, ahead of the others, and cloaked in black from head to toe, apparently ready to go to battle himself if it came to it. Logan guaranteed himself that it would, and that he would win, no question about it. He was clapping sardonically as a way of faux praise for the men for their accomplishment in defeating the lower levels of soldiers who were used ideally to weaken them and have them fully sapped before meeting their true match. "Gentlemen…and lady don't let me forget, I must say you have done a mighty fine job of taking out soldiers who wouldn't hold their own against a high school fencing class. I hate to be the bearer of bad news, but that was the hors d'oeuvre. Welcome to the appetizer." He held his hands aloft to welcome the hunters into the room and they entered as if they were in total control, egos as big as mountains. Logan thought only about how much he wanted to shut them up and deflate the sense of self they carried.

Jaguar was the first hunter in and he was followed by Grizzly, then Piranha, and finally Shark. It was too perfect in Logan's mind that there were four of them and his team was left with exactly four to face them. There was no way to know who each would be stuck fighting, but the reality was that each member of his team would be matched with one member of the opposition and how they chose was anyone's guess.

"Enough talk, motherfuckers! It is time for action," said Blue, angry and ready to vent some of it on these bad men who he had seen do awful things in a short time. They had rules and ideas, sure, but they were not as responsible about them as other people, often moving the goalposts to make a rule work in their favor.

That was all they needed to hear. Piranha threw down his katanas, Grizzly ejected his knives from his hands, and the others dropped their weapons as well. Piranha went for Blue, the one with the big mouth who liked to run it constantly, Grizzly edged toward Torrance, Shark approached Pink, and Jaguar, the most elite of the elites, went right for Logan.

While the rest of the team fought valiantly with their foes, Logan engaged Jaguar and had never felt so unequally matched with an opponent of any kind. He had fought professional fighters, he had taken on elite warriors all over the world, and he had even fought a man known as the 'toughest man in America' and it never felt like it did at that moment. The closest he had ever come to feeling the same way was in a fight with multiple bodyguards of a pop singer's rival who he had pissed off at a concert. Even then, he had defeated them easily since his overall skill aptly outshined theirs.

Jaguar placed a fast roundhouse kick to the side of his head and it sent him reeling. Logan hit the wall and then bounced to the floor. Dazed, he jumped back to his feet, and as soon as he was stable, the big man dug a closed fist into his abdomen that forced him to bend over completely and that was when Jaguar nailed him under the chin with an uppercut that sent him on his ass. He hit and then rolled over his neck and onto his feet in one constant motion. He staggered to his center and then attempted a kick to Jaguar's midsection that he caught with one hand and then attacked the leg with a vicious elbow that cracked bone. Logan cried out, but he couldn't let it get the best of him.

Able to rest only a little weight on his right leg, he tried planting it and spinning, landing his first blow, a roundhouse to Jaguar's shoulder since he was so tall. It rocked him, but he kept his balance. He swept Logan's leg and he was once again in control. With Logan on his back, he stomped his gut, whisking the air out of his lungs. He took in a deep gasp and then tried in vain to stand. Jaguar pressed his massive foot onto his chest and kept him down with ease.

Logan was running out of options, so he tried something he wasn't sure his injured back or other parts would allow. He pulled up his left leg as far as it would go and got it just in front of Jaguar's right. With his right already on the outside of Jaguar's left, he placed his left leg between the man's two open ones and locked them in a tight grip and rolled, taking the man down where he smacked his face on the floor hard. His mouth and nose both broke open and spewed blood.

Logan leapt up and climbed onto his back where he was able to grab Jaguar's head and lift-slam-repeat with it into the hardwood floor. His head was harder than Logan anticipated and it only pissed him off that Logan was doing it. He bucked like a bull and Logan fell off and Jaguar went for him like never before. He grabbed his throat and held it tight while he smashed his face into pulp. Logan was only able to break the grip by placing both arms by his chin and forcing them outward with all the strength he could gather. The second the grip was broken, Logan jumped and placed both feet squarely into his chest, pushing him back several feet before his slipped and fell. He was too quick for Logan to spring on, so he waited for him to come back at him.

Jaguar didn't disappoint, darting right for him as soon as he made it to his feet. He swung his full arm as hard as he could and connected with Logan's neck on the left side and he saw nothing but black for a mere second. It was just long enough that the attacker was able to feverishly ambush him with punches, kicks, and headers to various parts of the body. Logan felt like he was being run over by a plethora of different vehicles. With his sight restored and Jaguar thankfully growing tired, Logan was able to finally dominate the fight.

Logan thrust his fist into Jaguar's midsection over and over again, and the man stumbled, groaning in pain. When he had him on his heels, he kicked him hard in the same spot he had been pummeling, and the man fell to the ground with intensity. There was no time for him to cushion the fall with any part of his body. He hit on his back and bounced ever so slightly. Logan dashed over and dropped a knee into his chest, stealing his oxygen and sending him into gasping fits.

Logan was done playing and he was ready to finish off the fight. He pressed down on the man with all of his weight, holding him firmly to the floor with one knee on one hand and the other on the chest. He held the other wrist with his own hand. He pulled out a long, sharp knife and placed it to his throat, ready to slice it from ear to ear. "You fought hard, you fought well, but I told you from the start: I am going to win this. Don't feel bad. I haven't lost yet when it mattered."

"Great fight. Now, do what you have to do. I wanna go out like a man, motherfucker! Finish me!"

"With those words, Logan ripped the serrated blade across his skin and opened a gaping wound that drained of blood like a small waterfall. There were occasional spurts and then just dripping as all of the life finally drained out of him. Jaguar lay there dead and Logan stood, victorious, and took a deep breath. All around him, fights were still going strong and there was no way to gauge a winner or a loser in any of them. Logan locked eyes with Nestor.

The tall, muscular man was waving him over as he removed his black jacket. Logan was less than prepared to endure another battle, but this was the prize. This was the man he had wanted since the moment he said that he would have to kill his own family to be part of the organization. The feeling intensified when he had watched the motherfucker kill his daughter. He had felt some urge when he saw his wife's condition, but nothing like watching Anisa meet her untimely demise at the end of the barrel of his pistol. Right now, he was literally having difficulty restraining his building rage.

The large man stepped forward and without warning punched Logan right in the center of his face, breaking his nose. Logan recoiled but he was not expecting the brutality with which Nestor overwhelmed him. It was ruthless. He jumped on him and pounded him in the face with what felt like sledgehammers. He hit him so hard that his regular flesh split in multiple spots and blood poured from the wounds. With his fists bloodied from the attack, Nestor was shooting it in all direction with every retreat of his arm. He surprised Logan when he kneed him in the groin and pushed him backward onto the ground. Lying on the floor stunned, Logan was not anticipating the man using his gut as a literal stomping ground. He stomped on it several times, and Logan was breathless after the first. He kicked the leg as hard as he could, but with no air, there was no power behind it.

Nestor moved away to catch his own breath for a different reason, and Logan caught his just enough to leap. He was able to wrest the big man to the surface and attack. He was having trouble seeing with his swollen nose and blackening eyes. He was dizzy, but he had to act while he was able. With his opponent unable to retaliate, Logan stood over him and kicked him in the head to weaken him more. His head shot to the side and lolled back. Logan dropped to his knees and laid into the man's face in the same way the man had done to him. He didn't let up. He made every blow count. He refused to let the man have another attempt to stop him. He would walk away the victor, and he didn't care the cost on his end.

His effort was not wasted as Nestor lost consciousness. He kept hitting him, letting out all of the fury and rage that had been building since day one. He let up only when he decided to save his energy and kick the man in the face over and over again. He once again made the strikes worth the exertion. When blood sprayed with each contact, he knew he had more than accomplished his goal of ending the man's reign of terror. He wasn't satisfied yet, so he took out his pistol and a clip and put them together. He emptied the clip into the enemy combatant lying before him. He didn't aim and the shells entered the body at random everywhere from the stomach and chest to the neck and the head. When he fired the last one, he let out a sigh of relief. He genuinely believed he had let out all of the pent up anger and it felt good. He felt good for the first time in a long time. But the combat wasn't over.

To both sides of him there was fighting. He was stunned when he looked over and saw something that he thought he would never see. He wished he could have been faster, that he could have been closer to her when it happened. He screamed when he saw the gun and knew what was coming next. He had seen it too many goddamn times. He had done it to people more times than he could count. Shark without hesitation fired three shots into Pink's head. Logan watched as her head exploded in a stream of gore. He wanted to rewind time and save her before it happened.

Torrance had heard the shots and stopped to see what was happening, and then screamed something that no one in the room expected. "Motherfucker! You killed my daughter!" He punched Grizzly and ran over and attacked Shark with a ferocity he rarely displayed. He ripped out his pistol and fired indiscriminately in the man's direction. He hit him several times in vital spots and felled him. He collapsed to the floor dead as a doornail, and Torrance turned the weapon on Grizzly, ready to end what was a fair competition for a short time. He took aim this time, intentionally hitting the man in the chest, gut, and head. The only man left standing now was Piranha, and Blue was losing badly to him.

Logan fired a shot in the floor near the two rolling around on the ground. They stopped and separated. Blue looked angrily at Logan. "Stop! Everyone!" They looked at him. "This is over. Nestor, the Komodo is dead and that's the end of this!"

"What?" asked Piranha, confused by what he was hearing. "Over? You are letting me go?"

"Yes," said Logan coldly. "There is nothing left of the Animal Kingdom and you don't pose a threat here. It is three against one. I could kill you now and feel nothing."

"Fine, then I am getting the fuck out of here," said Piranha. He got up and just left without anyone trying to stop him. Blue and Torrance were both shocked at Logan's decision, and they wanted to stop the killer but they could easily have been killed too.

When he was gone, Logan turned to walk out as well. He got all the way to the door when it was slammed from behind. He didn't know what to make of it, but when he tried to open it and it was slammed again, he knew something was not right. He looked behind him at Torrance and Blue with guns in his face. "What the fuck?" asked Logan.

"You really have no idea do you?" asked Torrance. "All this time, and you never figured it out. So simple and you remain so blind."

"What the fuck are you talking about?"

"You are smarter than we thought you were, but this is putting the skids on that thinking," said Blue. "I cannot believe that you thought it was going to be that simple. We don't wipe slate clean, you stupid fuck! We make people pay their goddamn debts."

"I paid it. I did what you wanted."

"Ha, you are so naïve, Aster. You did a few jobs and you think that absolves you of sinking my organization for a decade?" asked Torrance.

"It was the agreement we had, you lame fuck!"

"I needed you to buy it and you did. I did your bidding if anything, and now it is time to pay for what you did to me."

"I was a fucking kid! You have to be able to understand that! You made mistakes when you were young, same as anyone else. Why can't you let my mistake be just that?"

"You fucked me! Kid or not, you fucked me and my organization in an unforgivable way. The only way I forget it is you die and I consider the debt paid."

"Then I guess we have a problem," said Logan, and he threw the door open and ran out without stopping. No one followed him, and he got in the Mercedes they had arrived in and checked the backseat for the bag he needed. It was secure in the floorboard. He drove off in the direction of nowhere, only some place he could go and be safe from the latest betrayal. He saw the ocean and could only think about how wonderful it would be to relax there if he had a normal life. He pressed the accelerator and left the house in the rearview and stared only at the road ahead, not knowing what lie there, but certain that it was going to get worse before it got better. Such was the life he had chosen.

CHAPTER FOURTEEN

Logan had made it to North Carolina where he stopped at a hotel on the beach and was able to finally take the breath he so desperately needed. It was called Beachfront Imperial Inn and he stayed in the farthest corner of the highest floor, away from everything and everyone. It was a master suite with a single queen-sized bed and a complete kitchen. He was prone to ordering food from room service, so the kitchen was unnecessary, but the bed was a welcome sight. He threw himself on it like it was a swimming pool and sank into it much the same way. He hadn't felt anything so soft or comfortable since he was still living at home with his wife and daughter. This bed actually made the one at his home that he had spent a lot of money to purchase, feel like a cot in field training for the military.

He fell asleep in a semblance of peace he had not known for quite some time and woke only when he was fully rejuvenated. Every section of his body was aching in one way or another, but he was able to ignore it with the renewed strength and adrenaline coursing through him. He didn't know what was in store for the days ahead, but he was elated he was able to face it with complete focus.

In the trunk of the car were weapons he would no doubt need soon, and in the floorboard of the backseat was the bag with Anisa's ashes that he would be dealing with when all of his troubles, including the newest ones, were officially done. He had spent far too little time thinking about the trick pulled on him by Torrance and Blue. It made less sense than anything else considering the genuine risk to their lives they had endured for his sake. They had nearly died countless times, and too many of Torrance's men to count had lost their lives in the service of a bullshit fake deal between Diamond Cartel and him.

He was flabbergasted that Torrance had let it get as far as it had gone, and he wondered to himself now sitting at the dining room table sifting through a room service menu why the fuck Torrance hadn't just killed him or had someone do it on one of the multitude of opportunities they had been given in their time together. He had never so much as suspected the deal was anything but sincere, and that was probably his own fault. He had grown much too trusting over the last few years, especially after having a kid and serving in the military. Thinking once again about what it was that led to the Diamond leader harboring such hatred for him caused him nothing but confusion. It was well established that he had caused chaos to the organization, but it was also well-known that he was young and following an order of a man who may or may not have known himself what he was doing to the group. He remembered being certain he was doing the right thing because that was how we was raised, but as he got older, he understood less and less about how much of what he was taught was right or wrong.

The waiter from the kitchen of the hotel arrived at the door with his order of a medium-rare steak with sweet potato fries, asparagus, and salad with Italian dressing. To drink he had ordered a simple large coke without ice, his normal go-to when it came to wanting a drink with a meal. He sat at the table to eat it and relax a little and was stunned by a buzzing in his pocket. He reached into it and withdrew his phone that he had literally completely forgotten about since it had gone unused for some time. He didn't recognize the number, but only a select few people had the number and most of them were not people a law-abiding citizen would just hand out their number too. He picked it up and answered it wordlessly.

"Oh, Logan," said Torrance delightedly. "I cannot believe you thought you were gonna get away from me just by running. Where did you think you were going, exactly?"

"I wasn't running, you insipid son of a bitch. I was recharging so I could be at full strength when I hand you and Blue both your asses."

"Oh, I see. Well, we are ready whenever you are, so come on down. And just as a little incentive to get you down here to Mexico, we have a little something for you." The air went momentarily dead and then a voice spoke that he was not expecting.

"Logan," cried Janet on the other end. "Help me. They are going to kill me unless you come here and finish what you started."

"You motherfuckers! You took my wife? Are you trying to make it worse for yourselves?"

"You know where to find us. You've been here. We look forward to seeing you again, really soon. Don't forget, you are on a deadline of two days."

"I will see you in one, you bastard!" screamed Logan. He threw his plate across the room and swept everything else from the table. So, Torrance was officially playing hardball. He wasn't going to make this easy and be a man and face Logan directly. He found the only weakness Logan had left and exploited it. The only thing the phone call had given him that he couldn't get on his own was Torrance's location. He lumbered across the room to his computer, provided by the hotel with internet access, and booked a flight to Mexico. He was about to engage in a one-man war, and he was more than ready to do just that.

Touching down in Mexico, Logan felt he was where he needed to be while also being in the place he least wanted to be ever again. It was a warm day, but weren't they all in this part of the world? Logan sat at the airport for the entire afternoon, sipping an ice cold coke and dwelling on the task to come. He was terrible at compartmentalizing ever since his life had come crashing down in spectacular fashion. It started with the job offer that went down the drain quickly, and then his wife was kidnapped, then his daughter was kidnapped and the man who raised him brutally murdered, and then his daughter was slaughtered right in front of him.

After downing the drink in its entirety, he walked to the exit. He didn't bring weapons on the plane. He shipped them to himself express and they would arrive later that day. He was anticipating their arrival because it meant he could go to work. Once out of the airport terminal he headed for the delivery service, in yet another rented, where he planned to wait until the package arrived. He refused to risk losing them to a misunderstood address or some other kind of translation fuckup.

He walked into the building and told the cashier what he was there for and was told it had not arrived. A check on its location said it was local and would arrive on the next truck within the hour. He took a seat, grabbed a magazine, and waited until the young woman told him that his box was there on the truck. It took longer than the aforementioned hour and Logan was upset at having to wait longer, but then she gave him the excellent news. "Mr. Gordon (his name for the shipment), your package has arrived."

Logan picked it up, signed for it, and left with it. He took it to the hotel where he set everything up the way he wanted it. He loaded rifles and handguns and donned the armor that would cover him from top to bottom, including his head. He was planning to dress much like the men he had fought in Florida. It hadn't worked out too well for them, but he wasn't them, so it was bound to end better.

When he was dressed and geared up, he packed the weapons case and carried it like a small suitcase and left the hotel using the rental. He drove the dirty, dusty streets that broke off from the main road at a pace even a grandmother could keep up with, considering the entire way just how he was going to approach the compound and men he encountered there. He planned to slip back into his persona of The Vapor, take out the exterior soldiers and then just disappear. He needed a plan to get inside, but the more he thought, the less of a clue he had about how that would happen. The easiest entry point would be the large gate, but there was no way for him to scale it without being seen. The other option was to parachute in, and that actually sounded like a wonderful idea in his head.

Coming around the final bend on a road adjacent to the one where the campus was actually located, he could see the building in all its glory. It stared him down like a menace with a grudge and he resented everything it was and stood for. More than anything, he hated that he needed to come back here especially to save the life of his wife. The last thing he wanted was to be put into this position, and he was sure he had relieved himself of it when he rescued his wife the first time. She had run off to god knows where and ended up in the hands of a completely different dangerous organization. "Jesus, talk about shitty luck," Logan said to himself out loud in the front seat of the car as he parked.

He climbed out and walked to a spot where he could see the whole area and took it all in. he knew what he needed to do, so he set up his rifle on the stand and worked with the settings until they were ideal. He would only need to adjust them for distance or wind, and then he could take out anyone within a few thousand meters. It could be a while before he acted, but he took up his position on the ground, staring at the open, empty space through the scope of the rifle.

A lot of time passed, and then there was activity. It started as a small buzz of one or two men, and then erupted into more than a dozen, and then twenty. Logan didn't know where they had come from since Torrance had mentioned previously that he was down to only the elites. He stared them down, wondering how many he could get before they grew wise to his location. He could easily take out more than ten, but that still left half of them with his location and a serious antipathy.

He was tired of letting his do the thinking about what he wanted and let the rifle do the talking instead. He took aim at the first head he had in view and corrected for distance. He poised himself and then pulled the trigger. The shot went unheard, but everyone saw the explosion of skull and blood as he fell to the ground. This was followed by running and screaming about getting out view and taking cover. When they had settled a little, he picked his next target and downed him. Before the men were able to react, he sighted several others and took them out as well. He had eliminated six of the twenty-two threats but that left far too many to make it easy on him.

After so many rounds from the same spot, he had been marked and the guns from that side were now aimed at him. He prepared himself for the barrage he was sure was coming, and despite being armored, it was going to be the equivalent of hundreds of wasp stings, and he hated being stung as much as anyone. When the first one hit, he could ignore it. He absorbed it and winced a little. The rest came at a stunning rate and he could do nothing more than lower his head into the ground and accept the discomfort of the stings.

When the bombardment was over, he was feeling them but he was able to deal with it. He was certain the opponents thought they had finished him, so taking more shots would be a mistake. He chose instead to creep across to the compound and sneak inside. It would take some doing, but he was sure he knew how he was going to do it. He remembered what Torrance had said about a vulnerability in the structure, so all he needed to do was find it. He went to the farthest end of the property where there were no guards visible and searched for anything that he might exploit. He got lucky more quickly than he expected when there was broken area of fence that he broke open further and slipped through.

Once inside, he maneuvered slowly around the building to a location form which he could see the remaining guards. He whipped out a small pistol and placed a silencer on it. When he got someone in view, he quickly fired, felling five more before he fled to a new place. The final eleven were going to be a challenge since he was running out of ways to snipe without being caught. He found one other spot from where he could go unseen and used it to his advantage. He climbed to the top of a small shed and stayed on the back slope of the roof. He peered over only when he was aiming to shoot. He was looking down on the group of guards who were looking all over for whoever was taking out their fellow soldiers. He ably took out seven of the last eleven. He tried to fire twice simultaneously but that was the biggest error in his judgement on the mission to that point. He was spotted and the men ran to the shed to meet him, and they were pissed.

Within seconds he was surrounded at the base by the only four soldiers left, and they were determined to finish him off. They shot at him on the roof, but with every bullet that met its target, they realized how fruitless an effort that was going to be. He waited until the exhausted themselves with the attempt and then leapt down to the ground like a twisted version of a superhero, even landing in a kind of pose, although accidentally. They only stared in confusion just long enough for him to react.

+++

In what could only be called an office inside the building, Torrance sat with Blue and Janet, who was tied to a metal chair in the center of the room. Her feet were tied to the two front legs and her wrists to the arm rests. She was blindfolded and gagged as well. On the table was a small handgun in front of Torrance and a rifle and large knife in front of Blue. They were both expecting Logan at any time, and they were as prepared as they thought they needed to be. He would, they both knew, make it in there sooner rather than later, and they would have to kill him to make him really stop coming after them.

"Boss, do you think he will come?" asked Blue, ready to go on the offensive but not quite willing to wait much longer to do so.

"Yes, he will be here. We have his wife. As far as he knows, she could already be dead or in serious danger, and he is not the kind to let people who hurt the ones he loves to walk away scot-free. I have seen it firsthand."

"If you want him so badly, then why are there twenty guards and soldiers outside waiting for him?" asked Blue.

"Well, he can't actually know we want him here. If it was easy for him to make it past the gate, then what reason would there be to think he wouldn't suspect something?"

"I don't know. He is not stupid. You told him you were out of men and now there are twenty of them out there to stop him. He is going to be suspicious."

"Yeah, I suppose so. But, he has to know that men are cheap and always for purchase. How hard would it be to buy two dozen and pay them to guard my camp?" asked Torrance.

"I guess you're right, boss, but I wouldn't put it past him to be wondering why went out of your way to buy men to impede him from the one thing you asked him to do."

"Why don't you shut the fuck up, Blue, and let me run shit the way I want? I know what I am doing, and if you don't like it, then you can go outside and deal with him without the protection offered in here."

"I am not arguing with your practices, boss. I am simply asking why you think it's necessary to throw such a roadblock in front of him when he came here to do what you asked him to."

"As I said, I cannot make it too easy. He has to work for what he wants," Torrance said, pointing to Janet as he did. "If he wants her badly enough, he will stop at nothing to get in here and get her."

"Okay, well how will we know when he is here?" asked Blue.

There were sounds in the courtyard at the same time he uttered the words and they both knew it meant only one thing. He was out there and he was causing bedlam on an extraordinary scale. The sounds were mostly gunshots, but that didn't mean much to either of them. The men could be shooting him, but it could most definitely and more probably be that he was shooting them. Torrance decided to look.

Walking over to the window that looked down on the property, Torrance could see that there were only a few men left and they were engaging a man dressed all in black armor. He had no doubt it was Logan, and he refused to watch his new fighters be handed their asses with such ease. He closed the curtain and sat back down. Blue looked at him with questioning eyes.

"What is it, boss?" he asked.

"Aster is here. He will be inside in no time. Take your position in the foyer downstairs and I will deal with him if he makes it this far."

Blue left without another word to go take his place in the foyer where he would greet Logan on his entrance into the building. Torrance stayed in his office area and awaited the impending defeat of Blue his own personal encounter with the man in an offensive showdown.

Standing to his full height, Logan was face to face with four soldiers of his newest, greatest enemy, and all he wanted was to get past them so he could be in the presence of Torrance and put an end to him as well. The more he thought about it, the more he wanted to leave them alone since they were new hires and didn't even know why he was here, and go in that building and face off with Blue and Torrance. He knew realistically that he couldn't do that and almost felt bad that genuinely innocent people were going to have to die to help him achieve his goal. He had felt bad, sort of, when he was doing with a gun from a distance, but being able to reach out and touch them, to end them by his own hands, made it more personal and in some ways more difficult. Perhaps he was growing too soft in his older age.

He swiped at the man closest to him and connected with his left cheek using his right fist. The man stumbled and another ran forward in his defense. Logan swung and hit him as well, knocking him to the ground. The third man and fourth man attacked together, one from the front and one from the back. Despite the injury to his back, Logan tried a move he hadn't attempted in so many years it was nearly impossible to count. He jumped up, kicked one leg forward and the other backward, with his front leg catching the attacker in the throat and the back one hitting a little lower, connecting with the attacker's stomach. Both of them fell with the momentum and direction of the kicks and Logan was once again harassed by the other two.

They came at him and one speared him while the other dove onto him and laid into him with punch after punch. All he could feel was the tightness and thickness of the armor and caused no damage. Logan let him tire himself out, much like the rope-a-dope pulled by Muhammad Ali in 1974 when he allowed George Foreman to exert himself and then began his assault. Logan, following the same formula, threw the man easily and then jumped up. He bombarded him with both fists, bloodying his face and breaking bones. The man gave up but Logan wasn't willing to give him a chance to come back at him. He snapped his neck and then moved on.

The man who had speared him was now waylaying him with kicks and punches, and Logan was parrying each one. It was almost too easy for him. The man was growing frustrated and throwing harder punches. He grew weak and exhausted so Logan finished him off the same way he had the other. Having two more assailants to deal with, Logan ran at them both. He was ambushed by one while he dealt with the other. The blows were like being in a bumper car at the carnival, and he easily ignored them. Logan trounced the man with several blows to his head with his arm and not his fist. Each hit made it harder for him stay standing and the final one had him without cognizance on the ground. He stood on the man's throat while he took out the other threat. He parried the blows once again, and this time he grabbed the leg in the course of a kick and raising his own right leg, he held it with his left hand and came down on it with all the power he could. He listened to the leg snap and the man fell backward screaming and writhing. He stepped once, hard, on the man's throat beneath him and then walked over to the one acting like a headless chicken. He lifted him, put one arm around his throat and pulled on it with his free hand. He held it until he heard a crunch and then he went to the ground lifeless.

He was thinking about them and how they didn't have to die as he walked toward the building housing Blue, Torrance, and Janet. He felt sorry for them, knowing they had been convinced or connived into working for a man as dishonest as Israel Torrance. He couldn't wait to rip his head from his shoulders with his bare hands, but he resented that he was able to manipulate yet another crop of trained soldiers and human weapons into doing his bidding that he was far too much of a pussy to try and do on his own.

He opened the new, thick oak door to the building and stepped inside into the familiar large room. He had taken only a single step inside when the round hit him and threw him back out the still-opened door. It took him a moment to orient himself. The blast had come from a large-caliber weapon, though rifle or handgun or something else, he didn't know. He rubbed his chest where the impact was made. He couldn't feel anything, but he knew when he saw it that there would be at the least a massive bruise.

Walking back inside, he steeled himself for another blast, and he was not disappointed. It hit him in the stomach and he fell forward this time since he was positioned differently, but it still hurt like being hit with a hammer. He rolled out of the way in case Blue decided to fire again, but luckily Blue was professional enough not to come after a man who was down. He saw Blue's shadow and he was carrying a large rifle. "Don't be a pussy! Put that down and fight me like a fucking man!"

"I plan to. This is just to let you know I'm here and I am ready to rumble. Warning shots, if you wanna think of them like that," said Blue.

"I am warning you, motherfucker. Put that down or I will make it worse for you."

"I'll be there in a second. Be patient. Damn!"

Blue came on him with the rifle raised and pointed directly at his head. His finger was caressing the trigger and Logan knew he had plans to use it, and his thoughts about professionalism all took a needed back seat. Blue looked at him hard with dark eyes. Logan had never noticed how evil the man could look when he wasn't on your side. He cringed a little involuntarily.

"Here I am, you son of a bitch. And I am gonna fuck you up!" said Blue.

Logan, without warning, kicked Blue's leg out from beneath him, causing him to lose his grip on the rifle that skidded away as a result. He stumbled but kept his feet. It was enough of a window for Logan to reach his feet and roundhouse him to the head, coming completely off the ground to do so. All the pain he was feeling was sent to another place for the time being. The kick leveled Blue and as Logan ran over, Blue used his right leg to sweep both Logan's legs and drop him to the ground as well. They both stood at the same time, like a performance.

Logan darted for Blue who expected it and caught him by the waist and pushed him to the ground face-first. His head hit and bounced, and Blue knelt down, picking it and slamming it several more times. The visor of the helmet broke and thick glass went everywhere. Logan bucked and pushed him off, turning over and removing the broken helmet. Blue was getting back up when Logan stood and kicked the man in his chest, sending him flying backward. He hit a wall and then slumped forward. Logan rushed him, pushing him up against the wall once again will full force. While there, he battered his face with his fists. The wounds poured blood into the floor and all over Logan, but he continued. "Die, motherfucker!" screamed Logan.

"Enough!" screamed Blue. "You win!"

"Fuck you!" returned Logan. He grabbed Blue by the collar and threw him roughly to the floor. He landed with a loud knock and slid a little. He was motionless but still breathing and conscious. Logan walked over and leveled several kicks into his midsection. Blue curled up and writhed in pain. Logan then kicked him in the face. It split like a ripe melon and gushed even more blood. Blur grabbed his face to see how bad it was and came back with a hand and arm full of red liquid. "Stop! I don't wanna die!" he screamed.

"I don't care. You betrayed me. Betrayal has consequences and you have to pay them!" Logan pulled out his handgun and placed it to Blue's head. He feebly pushed it away and it was replaced. This happened again, and he gave up entirely. Logan pulled the trigger twice, putting two holes in the side of his head. He stood up and put three more into his chest, each one pumping the body as if it was being defibrillated. "Torrance, you fuck! Where are you? I'm coming for you next!"

+++

Torrance heard the commotion downstairs and became more worried than he thought he would be when it came town to stare down his nemesis. It sounded like a small-scale battle in the foyer, and he wasn't sure if that was good for Aster or for Blue. When he heard the screams of a familiar voice, he knew then that Blue was the one in danger, and Logan was getting the upper hand. As he heard more sounds of an imperiled man, he couldn't help but have a tinge of fear run up his spine. He didn't really know how dangerous Logan would be to him personally because he had never faced off with him. Everything he had seen him do to other people perpetuated the idea that he was not to be messed with, but it was different when he was after you personally.

The unmistakable sounds of gunfire really made Torrance's heart beat faster than that of a person on cocaine (and he had been there), and he didn't like the feeling one bit. Janet had squirmed a bit at hearing the shots because there was no way she could have known that they were from her husband who was on his way up in a matter of seconds to rescue her. Torrance recoiled when he heard his name. He knew without any more doubt that Logan had dispatched Blue and was coming for him. He was desperate to end Aster once and for all, but he wasn't as sure as he had been that it would be that simple. Blue was a force to be reckoned with and Logan had taken him out of commission in a matter of minutes from the time the first shot was fired with the rifle.

He could hear steps outside the room on the stairs leading to the level his office was on, and then they were coming down the hall. He was opening every door he passed and slamming it as evidence he was in the vicinity. With each one he said two words that he saying in a loud tone to make sure Torrance heard them, and was hopefully terrified by them. "Getting closer!"

He could hear doors closer to him opening and closing and it was putting him on edge. He understood now that he was far from ready to engage with the monster coming down the hallway. When he saw the knob turn, he winced. It was locked, but there was no way a man that determined was going to let something as simple as a lock keep him from his destination. He was right and he knew it when the door buckled several times due to kicks on the area around the knob and striker. The final one, the seemingly strongest of all of them, busted it free and it flew open, smashing against the wall inside the room. The man Torrance now feared instead of felt superior to, stood there in all black, with a look on his face that could kill by itself. He withdrew quickly.

+++

Logan stood boldly in the doorway, staring at the tall man who had changed his life, but decidedly not for the better. He moved a single step toward Torrance when the man stared back and tried in vain to look menacing. He had that power over Logan once, but that was before he had angered him in a way he had never himself even known before. One quick way to get a person on your bad side was start kidnapping the people they cared about. A quick way to make them your worst nightmare was to kill the person they loved most. Torrance had taken Anisa from Logan and it was the biggest mistake he had ever made. Logan looked at him now and he knew his death was imminent.

"Glad you made it," said Torrance with a shaky voice. "I wasn't sure we would see you here in time."

"I'm not here to talk. I am here for my wife, and that's it. Once I get her, I am out of here."

"Too bad she isn't going anywhere then, isn't it?" asked Torrance.

"I don't plan to save her until I kill you, so there is time for her to get ready."

"You have to get through me before you can get to her, and I don't think you have what it takes to do that."

"I guarantee you, I have what it takes. Ask Blue, or any of the other dead soldiers out there. All twenty-three of them will gladly testify to the fact that I cannot be stopped. You can ask them when you take your ass to hell to meet them."

"I can offer you the same message. Tell them when you arrive," said Torrance.

"I didn't come here to talk, you evil fuck! I came here to get my wife back." He ran at the man unexpectedly. He picked him and slammed him down on the table in a mixture of strong man and wrestling move. The tabletop cracked from the impact and then collapsed. Torrance groaned and then tried to stand. He was wobbly-legged and couldn't quite right himself. Logan gave him the chance to do just that. He wasn't going to kill a man who was so out of sorts. Torrance finally got his bearings and stood in a fighter's stance.

Torrance's left foot was facing Logan, slightly bent with his right leg behind him bent a little more. His left arm was extended before him, bent at the elbow and his right arm was bent as well, but instead of being balled in a fist, it was open in a chop position. He was ready for punches, and maybe kicks, but he was less than prepared for what Logan tried. He dashed at him and tackled him at the knees, forcing him to the ground where his head smashed against the table leg. Torrance cried out in pain and Logan felt a touch of pride. When Torrance stood up again, he got back into his stance.

Logan came at him as he expected this time and the result was what it should have been. Logan punched at him and he deflected it, then landed one of his own on Logan's left cheek. His head jerked to the side and then it was followed by a flurry of whacks that all rocked his head from side to side. After the final one, Torrance kicked him in the gut and doubled him over, not in pain, but as a reaction to the blow itself. As Logan was bent over, Torrance brought up his knee into his forehead and knocked him backward to the floor. He hit and slid several feet on the smooth surface. His face was teeming with blood.

Logan wasn't granted the same right as Torrance and given time to get right before his oppressor attacked. Torrance went right at him again, this time kicking him in the ribs and chest, causing Logan to curl into a ball to stem the impact. He was finally able to catch one foot as it came flying in and he pulled it to himself and then thrust it with all his might, toppling the tall man. He leapt to his feet and pounced. He leveled countless thumps to the face before Torrance swept his feet with a well-placed movement. When he fell, Logan rolled and jumped back to his feet. Torrance did the same.

Both men on their feet, Logan went to a move he was confident with. He put his weight on his left foot and spun on the ball of it, swinging his right foot around at a height even with Torrance's head, and connected just above his jawline. The roundhouse kick brought down the man with ease. He lay on the ground with some dizziness for longer than was suitable. Logan was tired of waiting for him to be prepared so he dove on him and gave him one strong elbow to the face that sent him into blackness.

Logan rushed over to the chair where Janet was tied tightly. Well, it was more than ties. She was bound with some kind of cord Logan had never seen before. It was almost like a metal that could be tied and knotted. There was no way in hell he could untie it with his hands, so he had to go and find something. He ripped the blindfold off of her eyes and saw that she had been crying a lot. The redness was something he only saw after he and her, or she and Anisa had a row that caused her to freak out. Next, he tore the gag from her mouth, expecting some kind of a reply, but she gave him nothing. He was stunned at how sad she looked. It didn't make a lot of sense that she wouldn't be happy to see him, but he chocked it up to her intense state of shock. He ran from the room and searched as many rooms as he needed to in order to locate something he figured would do the trick. He found three things to try and then hurried back to his wife's holding room. She was still not speaking or moving. She just wanted to be free.

The first item he tried was a garden-variety chef's knife but was a little longer than any he had personally used in a kitchen while cooking. He put all his effort into it and it did him no good. He couldn't even force a dent into the odd material. He kept trying, but coming up empty with every attempt. He got frustrated and tossed the knife across the room where it landed after hitting a window. The next item he tried was a pair of shears with platinum blades. With these he was able to forcefully cut a small tear in one of the binds, but it was not going to cut all the way and it sure as shit was not going to be effective for all of them. The final object he had that he thought would be effective was a scary little laser like device he had found in a room filled with discarded equipment. He assumed the stuff came from the old room where he had first met Torrance to set up the deal he had never been serious about. He took the laser and let it get hot. It emitted a beam that he tested on a couple of spots not touching her skin first to see how it would act. It cut it like a heated knife would cut through butter. He moved to the more sensitive areas making contact with the skin and raised them as much as he could away from the flesh to give himself room to operate. He was able to get them all off of her with little effort and almost no burns. She was free but still in shock, she didn't move a muscle.

Logan reached over and held and hugged her and she put her arms around him, lightly at first, and then she grabbed him and squeezed so tightly that it took his breath away for a slight second. She wasn't speaking and he didn't know why, but he wanted to hear her voice. "Baby, it's Logan. Can you hear me?" he asked.

"Y-y-y-yes," she stammered. "I h-h-h-hear you."

"You are free now. We can get out of here. Let's go."

"I c-c-c-can't go w-w-with y-y-you."

"Yes, sweetie. Of course you can. We can leave right now." He tried to lift her from the chair and she refused to budge. He was more than a little confused but he thought that maybe her legs were not working from being tied up for so long.

"N-n-n-no, I can't." She darted to her feet, ripped the handgun away from his waistband and pointed it right at his head. "Sit the fuck down, Logan!"

CHAPTER FIFTEEN

Logan looked at his wife more confused than he had ever been in his life. He sat down, but he had no idea what was happening. He was more surprised when Torrance came up, awake from his too-short slumber from an elbow to the face. He grabbed Janet and hugged her and she smiled. Logan was beside himself with confusion now. There was nothing harder to believe than what he was actually seeing with his own eyes. He wanted to ask questions, but they were not about to answer anything he had to ask. There was no way he could begin to wrap his head around it. The more his thoughts went to it, the more perplexed he became. More than anything else, it was the hug and smile that sticking with him. How the fuck did those two know each other and why the fuck would they be conspiring against him together?

She still held the handgun aloft pointed at Logan's head. Torrance was now tying his hands and feet to the chair exactly as Janet's had been. The only difference, he told himself, was that this was not going to be pretend. This was going to be the real thing, and there was nothing he could do to prevent it. He had never so quickly or seriously regretted letting a target, one marked for certain death, escape for even a short time. He had planned to kill him on the way out of the room after his wife was safe and secure. He was appalled at how and how fast that had all backfired and turned into whatever the fuck this had become.

Now bound to the chair, Torrance was placing a gag in his mouth and then wrapping it with a strong cloth of some kind. He couldn't speak if he wanted to, and that was usually a sign from a torturer that you needed to listen rather than talk. He next put the same blindfold around his eyes that had been on Janet's only a short time ago. With his hands, feet, mouth, and eyes tied or covered, immobile and unusable either way, Logan felt that he had made a huge mistake. Not in letting Torrance live so much, although that would nag him until his dying breath. It was more about how coming here had always been the last thing he wanted, and now he understood to a larger degree why. He already knew the asshole couldn't be trusted, so what had made him think that leading him here was going to end any differently than with the same dishonesty that had been the motive for the man the entire time? He felt stupid about not realizing he was walking into some kind of trap, at the least. He felt ridiculous for not knowing that things were definitely not as clear-cut as they seemed. Now, he was close to dying for his mistakes, and for the first time in his life, he felt like he deserved death. Not because of things he had done. He could always justify those. Rather, because he had let himself fall into the trap he was in now, and all he could think was that he was losing his touch, losing a grip on who he once was and what he was able to do. Death was pertinent.

Torrance looked at him hard, but then remembered he was blindfolded and backed off on the intimidation attempt. "You should have known better, Aster. I gave you no reason to trust me, but you came running like a boy with a lost puppy as soon as you believed your wife was in danger." He looked to see if Logan was making any kind of movements. He wasn't. All he was doing was sitting as still as a statue in the chair where he was losing his temper silently.

"Sweetie," said Janet. "It was by chance that we met, but when I learned the truth about you, it was all I could do not to kill you then."

"Yeah, it's a shame you couldn't hide your activities better. What kind of hitman leaves his job info for his wife to find? For that matter, what hitman has a fucking wife in the first place?"

"You never should have done what you did, and you definitely never should have let me find out. I mean, how would you feel if someone walked into your home and killed your parents? Oh, right! You had that happen too, didn't you?"

"She never told you her real last name. Why would she since she didn't have a living mom or dad? Would you like to know what her last name is? Let's ask her." He turned to Janet and with a sarcastic tone spoke directly to her. "Would you mind giving our contestant your actual name?"

Janet sighed, took in a deep breath and spoke sincerely. "Well, Logan, I told you my name was Janet Crowe. We can dispense with the lie now. My real name is Janet Dianne Sardis. My dad's name was Dustin Wayne Sardis and my brother was named Brady Elliott Sardis. You killed them both about twenty years ago."

""Did you know Pink was my only child, and you let her die, just like you did your own daughter? You are worthless at keeping those you care about alive. I saw the way you looked at her. You cared deeply. You don't know how lucky you are that she died. We had big plans for her that included getting close to you. I have no doubt you would have allowed it. Hmm, and it all comes full-circle, doesn't it? I am thankful that you fucked over the Animal Kingdom. They set a new plan in motion that nearly got you killed and saved me the trouble. When you told me who your wife was and that she had been taken, I hoped she would come back safely simply because she deserved to be the one to kill you," said Torrance.

"I have wanted to kill you from the moment I learned the truth, but the time was never right. It would have been suspicious and I couldn't serve life in prison without you suffering for what you did to my family. You killed my dad and brother, but what I didn't tell you was that my mom waited until I graduated from high school and went to college and then she killed herself because of the damage you caused us. You ruined our lives."

"It seems all of this is new information, and to put it in a way you can understand, it was another one of your little fuckups. You had the pure hatred of the Diamond Cartel and the daughter of your victim, all for the same killing. He gave you an opportunity for wealth, but you should know, should have known, that wealth always comes at a price."

"My dad was a good man. My brother was what every kid dreams of for a sibling. My mom was the best any child could ask for. You took that all away from me and now I am going to finally get to take away the thing you always cared about most: your own life."

"Yes, Aster. It all ends here. It was a valiant effort, but unfortunately you are at the end of the line. The only way you walk out of here now is with a miracle," said Torrance. He reached down and took off the gag and gave Logan a chance to speak. "Anything you wanna say before I allow your wife to carry out the execution?"

Logan looked where he thought they were and took in a deep breath. "I just wanna say that I am surprised by everything you said here today, but I want you to know that I have no plans to die in here or anywhere. Before I walk out that door, and I will, I am going to kill you both."

"I am genuinely curious about you plan to accomplish that," said Torrance.

"I'll show you." Logan stood quickly and rammed Torrance with the chair and he fell to the ground, landing on his side and screeching in pain. Before Janet could use the weapon, he charged at her and rammed her using his head and she fell backward, dropping the gun on her way down. Logan jumped as high as he could with the chair strapped to him and landed on the back of it on the hard floor. The pieces of metal bent but did not fully give. Janet was going for the gun once again and Torrance was coming to when he tried for a second time. This time the chair came apart. It was more cheaply made than the ties on his wrists.

He slid his arms and legs free of the chair parts and stood to his full height. Janet was coming at him and he slapped her hard in the hand, dislodging the weapon once again. He kicked her legs out from under her and she fell on her face. She screamed and then rolled around in agony. He caught Torrance with an elbow to the throat as he charged from behind. Janet was hurrying to retrieve the gun, but Logan was much too quick for her. He reached down and grabbed it and pointed it at her. "I loved you. I loved you with everything I had. I put my life and career at risk for you, and you betrayed me. Why not leave when you knew who and what I was?"

"I wanted to, but we had that stupid kid and you loved her and I didn't want to be the mom who ran out and left dad with a kid to raise. I wanted people to believe we were happy."

"Do you think anyone really believed that? We never showed anyone that. We never had anything to show people because we kept ourselves hidden from the world. I know now that all you wanted was to be close to me so you could kill me when the time came."

"Yes, that's what I wanted. I wish I had done it. You deserved it, and you still do. I still plan to kill you before you walk out of here."

Torrance had come up behind him and he felt a gun in his back. It wasn't a standard handgun. It was harder and the way he was pressing it, it felt like it was digging significantly deeper into the armor than the one he was carrying. "Listen up, Aster. The gun in your back is an invention by one of my men. It is not a typical firearm. This one holds armor-piercing rounds and I am not going to hesitate to fire one right into your liver if you fuck around."

"I don't care what you do to me, Torrance. I will kill her before you have a chance for a second shot and you will damn sure need two."

"I am willing to do that. You think I care if she dies? I brought her here to kill you. I have no stake in her life. If she dies, it is a risk she took by coming here."

"Fuck you, Israel. You told me you would help me to kill him, but if that's how you feel, maybe I just let him kill you too," said Janet.

"Both of you shut up! This is not going to end well for anyone here, but as it stands, I am prepared to die in my effort to kill you both, and neither of you are ready to die."

"I have had enough," said Torrance and pulled the trigger. Logan had moved ever so slightly and the bullet lodged in his right side, missing all of the organs. He felt the blood pool inside his armor and he felt weak, but he didn't falter. He turned swiftly, dropped his own gun and grabbed the gun from Torrance's hands before he knew what had happened. He looked horrified and Logan loved seeing it in his face. He pointed it at the older man and stared hard. "What the fuck was that?"

"It was supposed to kill you," said Torrance plainly.

"It didn't, and now I am going to kill you. All you had to do was not fucking shoot me and there was a chance you walked away."

Logan wasn't paying attention and Janet picked up his gun, pointing it at him with intent. She was angry and he could feel it, but he didn't even realize she was pointing a loaded gun at him. "Don't do it, Logan. He dies and you die." He turned his head and looked at her without moving his steady hands.

"Oh, shit. I forgot about that thing. You know what, Janet? Just fucking kill me already. Get it over with and let's call it a day."

"I don't want it to be that simple, Logan. You deserve to be punished for what you did. Suffering is what I want for you."

"It's not gonna happen, Janet. Keep in mind, I am not afraid to kill you, so I would lower that weapon and decrease that risk." He turned back to Torrance. "I am done with you. I tried to give you a chance and you betrayed me all over again. You even knew the whole time about my wife. You let me think I was saving her when all I was doing was giving myself up to your machinations."

"You are smarter than I would have thought, but if I am being honest, you are as stupid as shit when it comes to manipulating you with people you trust or care about."

"I will admit, I fell easily for your ploy, but I am prepared to rectify that right now."

"And how do pl-," he was cut off mid-sentence as Logan fired two shots in succession into his head and chest, sending him reeling. He was dead long before he hit the ground and when he did, he landed with a thwack and then never moved again. Logan ducked as soon as the second shot was fired, expecting Janet to pull the trigger in retaliation.

She fired twice, missing both with unprecedented inaccuracy from such close range. Logan stood up and kicked his wife's hand with all his strength. She lost the weapon for a third time. This time, he didn't give her an opportunity to get it again. He went right for her, punching and slapping her like she was any other target. She had caused it to happen to herself. He didn't care how it made him look. He kicked her in the stomach and roundhouse to the head. She fell over and then he picked her up and pressed her against the wall with force. She was scared now, knowing death was a real possibility. He was not prepared to let up because she was still aware and had begun fighting back. She was thrashing and kicking at him. She caught him in the gut but he was still wearing the armor. He winced when she got him square in the spot he had just been shot. He wanted to cry out, but he refused to give her the satisfaction.

He was growing weary of the whole thing, and he just wanted to be done with it. He was willing to walk away without killing her. "I will let you live if you promise to give up this silly dream of getting revenge on me for something that happened twenty years ago. If you insist, then I will kill you and walk away as if nothing ever happened."

"I will never give up because you will never deserve anything less. You killed my whole family. I owe this to you."

"Do you even care that you own daughter is dead?" asked Logan.

"No, not even a little bit. Do you know how many times I wanted to do it myself and pretend she never existed? Hearing you say she was dead made me feel happier than I have in a long time."

"Well, I loved her and I will never accept that she is gone. I made a promise to her and if you kill me and I cannot fulfill that promise, then I swear to everything holy, I will haunt you until your dying day."

"If I have my way, and I plan to, the haunting should start today."

"If that's the way you want it," he said, dropping the gun at his feet. He grabbed her by her collar and threw her harshly to the floorboards where she landed with a horrible cracking sound. He picked her up and did it once more. She was limp on the floor and he left her there. He walked toward the door and was opening it when he heard the rustling.

He picked up the gun he had used to kill Torrance and turned around. Pointing his own gun at him was Janet. She was unsteady and each time she pulled the trigger it wasn't even close. With the final bullet, she was able to hit him in the chest. It slowed him down and pushed him back, but it didn't hurt him. Afraid that she was only proving her determination to kill him now or eventually, he did what he had to do. He pointed the gun at her, nearly blinded by the tears in his eyes, and fired it three times, hitting her squarely in the head and chest, a signature move for him. He watched the life drain out of her and he was sorry it had to come to that. He left her alive, giving her a chance to recant and let him live with the mistake he had made rather than making him die for it. She wasn't willing to do that, and he wasn't willing to let her live if she couldn't. Before he left, he pulled two grenades from a chest strap, ripped out the pins, and tossed them, one near her and one near Torrance. He left them behind and the explosions rocked the whole building as he took his final steps toward freedom that he didn't feel he had earned, but rather had obtained through extremely unfortunate circumstances. He was once again wiping away tears as he walked to the stolen Mercedes.

+++

They had never visited together and she had been a couple of times with her mother when she still somewhat cared about her, but Anisa had always said it was her favorite place to go. She had even said that when she was older she wanted to live there. As Logan drove his new car, a BMW, to the location, he was fighting tears for the umpteenth time in the last few days. He had cried for everything from his wife and her death at his hands to finally taking time to deal with the death of his daughter. He was not afraid to show his sensitive side to himself, though other people could never be allowed to see it. The view of the ocean from where he decided to park was one of the most beautiful things he had ever seen. The blue of the water so bright that it was blinding. There were boats and surfers on the waves and the breeze moved the treetops in a way that was mesmerizing.

He stepped out of the car and the breeze hit him like a welcome friend. He stood and just let it waft over him for a few seconds before walking down to the shoreline where he met the man who would be piloting his boat to the 'special' place Anisa was so set on. It was nothing more than a small island in the center of the water off of the California coast called nzuri zaidi asili, which was Swahili for what roughly translated to 'the most beautiful nature." It was the most gorgeous place Logan had ever been, and he had traveled the world more than once. Of course, he was usually in a location for reasons other than taking in the views.

He could understand why Anisa said things about wanting to live on the island when she was old enough to go out on her own. He was still a long way off from being able to dock the boat and walk on the sands, and he was considering what it might take to purchase a place there. He was enamored by the beauty, but it was more impressive to him how far it was from everything and how quiet it was. He had been encapsulated by near-silence for as long as he could remember. This was the closest to that he had been in a long time.

"Almost there, Mr. Aster," said the pilot, a man named Ian Forrester. "We will dock in about five minutes."

"Thanks, Ian," he said. "I appreciate the ride."

"It's no problem. I will be here when you wanna go back too."

Logan disembarked when the boat finally docked. He was stunned to see hotels on the small island. He couldn't see them from the water because they were not huge and mostly concealed by the tall trees. There were two of them, and each had about twenty rooms. They only had three floors with the rooms on floors two and three. The ocean could be seen from ever room in both buildings. He was half-tempted to book one for the night, but he had an appointment he absolutely could not miss early the following day.

He had a pack around his neck inside which was the urn containing Anisa's ashes. He wasn't ready to pull it out just yet, so he waited until he had walked around a bit. He wanted to get as much of the emotion out as he could before doing the most emotional thing he had done in his whole life. He saw a lot of people, but he didn't speak to any of them. That was the last thing he needed. He did lazily wave at a few of them who waved first, but that was as much interaction as he desired for the time being.

He walked to the edge of the water on the west side of the island and waited for the sun to set. It was nearing that time and he was sweating from the anxiety and fear of what he had to do. He was sad but he hid that much better than any of his other emotions. As soon as the sun was on its way down and before he did anything else, Logan recited the best poem Anisa had ever written that he ignored until she was no longer around.

"Days when I am happy or days when I am sad/every day I am alive I am thankful for my dad/he hasn't always been there to help me through/I know that there is nothing daddy wouldn't do/he cries like anyone else when he is sad/and even if he didn't he will always be my dad/no matter what tomorrow brings good or bad/I will always be thankful for the things I have had/more than anything else I will always be grateful for my dad."

He finally pulled out the urn and held it in his hands firmly. He clutched it to his chest for a brief second and then he held it aloft. He removed the top and while reciting the poem once again, with each stanza he dumped a little of the ashes at a time into the water. As planned, with the utterance of the last stanza came the last of the ashes. He watched them hit the water and then float away. In his mind it was too reminiscent of the brief nature of Anisa's life where she was here one moment and gone the next, and she was not coming back, the same way the ashes would follow the current and he would never see them again.

When the sun had vanished completely and it was growing dark, he went back to the boat where Ian was still waiting for him. He smiled at the pilot and climbed in. several minutes later he was docking and then walking away from the ocean. He turned one last time to look at the view and imprint a picture on his mind that he would never forget. "Goodbye, sweetheart. Daddy loves you."

Two years had passed since the final time Logan had seen his wife or his daughter, both dead now, more or less at the hands of the same person. He didn't want to blame himself for something so heinous, but he had been doing nothing but that for the last two years nonstop. He had been able to get back to work shortly after the final blow to his confidence when he had to kill his own wife to prevent her from eventually killing him. Instead of jumping back into murder-for-hire, he had done something more unlikely. He hired men and rebranded the Animal Kingdom as his own organization that was designed to carry out missions much like the old one, but with more of a code of honor. He considered it to be similar to the job the Equalizer did in the old television show. People would call him when they had something they couldn't handle alone and him and his men would deal with it for a fee. He called it Anisa's Hands, and he was getting calls daily from people who needed his help in one way or another, and business was going as smoothly as anyone could hope for.

He was sitting at his desk when his personal phone rang. It was a number not many people had, so when it rang, it usually meant something serious. He had not had to answer it in over two weeks, so he kind of looked forward to knowing who had something so urgent they used that number instead of the business phone. He pressed the green circle and said the only two words that came to mind. "Aster here."

"Mr. Aster, you don't know me. My name is….you know what? My name isn't important. I am calling to tell you that I have been looking for you since Able Lock died. I know you think you knew him, but what did you really know about him?"

"Look, I don't have time for this. I have a serious business to run. If you have something to tell me, then say it so I can get back to work."

"How much did you know about Lock? I bet he told you a lot stuff. I also bet none of it was remotely true. He lied about everything to us, so I can imagine he did the same to you."

"Who is this?" asked Logan, growing frustrated.

"I won't ask what he told you, exactly," said the man, ignoring Logan's question. "I can only assume it had something to do with…you know what? I said I wasn't going to pry so I won't."

"Who are you? Why are you talking about Able like you know him? He didn't have friends. Hell, he didn't even have acquaintances."

"I will only say this: he had a life before you came into his, and he knew your father for a reason. Take that how you will, do with it what you want, but I am trying to help you."

"How, in any way, is this helping me? You are telling me the man who raised me, who brought me up to be what I am, was not who I thought he was or even who he told me he was," said Logan calmly, surprising even himself.

"The only thing you need to do," said the man," is go to the house where he died. There is a hole in the kitchen floor. Under it is a room. Inside that room is the truth to everything. You have make sure you are prepared to find it before you go in. once you see it, it cannot be unseen and certainly not ignored."

"You know I am likely to go, and I am ready to prove you wrong. If I go, what can I expect to find?"

"The truth. Nothing more and nothing less."

"How will I know if I find what you're telling me about?"

"There will be no question. If you find it, you will know and it will change everything you thought was true."

"Fine. I will go, but if I don't find anything, I am going to be pissed that some nameless, faceless motherfucker wasted my time and took me away from my work."

"Fair enough, Mr. Aster. Let me up the ante. If you don't find it, you can be pissed all you want. If you do, then we will work together to solve a mystery you didn't even know existed."

"Fine. We have a deal. If I find what's there, I will work with you to solve whatever mystery it creates."

"I will contact you in one week at this number. Until then, good luck."

Logan was once again traipsing through the home of the man who had brought him up as his own. There was nothing the caller could have said that made him believe anything bad about the man. He had done everything he could to give him the life he so richly deserved after such a monstrous tragedy had befallen him at such a tender age. He had never lied to him about anything, so trusting the caller and coming here to investigate the possibility that he had was something he would never have done in the older days of his existence.

He was in the kitchen looking for some kind of hatch or other way into a secret room that already had doubts existed. He kicked things out his way, ran his hand all across the floor and found nothing. He was losing his patience and ready to walk out when he decided that it wasn't worth it to him to come all the way out here and leave assuming the caller was laying rather than knowing for certain that he was. He cleared the whole kitchen floor which took about half an hour even though all he did was throw stuff into the living room or onto the countertops. With only the bare floor beneath him, he knelt down on his hands and knees and placed his face to the floorboards, scanning the expanse with his eye and then moving to another location and doing it again. After trying from all four directions, he had seen only one commonality.

He went to the center of the room, kind of disgusted that it was so simple, and felt around for what he saw in his sightings as a small gap between floor and what appeared to be a small door of some kind. He touched a tiny fissure and then forced his fingers into it far enough to get under the bottom edge of it. He lifted up and a trapdoor the size of a car door came squeaking open. He pulled a little flashlight from his pocket and shined it into the abyss. A ladder dropped down from the top to the floor roughly eight feet below made of thick rope. He couldn't see any of the contents of the room, so he descended the ladder and entered it for himself.

There were nearly one hundred boxes that he had never seen and didn't have any clue were even in existence. They came in all colors and sizes, and he would have to rummage through all of them if he was to find what the mysterious caller was hinting at. He was already appalled that the caller knew about this and he didn't, but he couldn't waste any more time. He ripped off the top of the first box and dumped the contents in an empty section on the floor. He scoured them and came up with nothing of any substance. He continued doing it to the boxes one at a time. While he was sure he hadn't found what the caller was referring to, he had discovered more than a couple of things that made hi, angry. It was clear after only a tenth of the boxes that Able Lock was not the man he said he was. His name wasn't even Able Lock as far as Logan could tell. Several of the documents in the boxes had his name as something completely different: Harold Franklyn. He knew why the name sounded so damn cool now.

He was halfway through the boxes when it crossed his mind that there was not one thing to find. He was piecing together some sort of puzzle. The more pieces he found, the better he could understand it and the clearer it would be. He put aside everything that conflicted with something he was told and the stack grew immense quickly. He was learning that his name was a lie, his backstory was a lie, and his family life was a lie. It was box 56 that changed his whole world.

The picture was of Able (or Harold) standing with three boys. He was a little younger than when Logan had met him, but there was no disputing who it was in the image. Logan took a minute to place the men he was with but he had definitely seen them somewhere before. He thought hard about where and it just wouldn't come. He tossed the picture in a place he could locate it with ease and continued hunting through the contents. He found more stuff to add to the pile and none of it was really worth the call he had received. At the bottom of the box, however, there was a medical file that he had never seen in his life. He almost didn't want to open it, but he was convinced this was where he would find the evidence the caller had led him to.

Unsealing the cover from the first page ever so slightly at first and then forcing it all the way, he saw a picture he recognized. It was his sonogram from while his mother was pregnant with him. He had seen it a couple of times growing up. It even had his name on it. There was nothing about it that suggested anything odd except it was in Able's hidden room. He kept flipping pages and reading as he came to new ones.

He knew that he had found it. He couldn't even believe what he was reading, but it was there, signed by a doctor, and as much proof as he needed that it was true. The birth certificate said the father was Harold Franklyn, but Able never had kids of his own. Or that was what he had told Logan. It appeared to be just another lie. The mother was listed also, and her name was Samantha Freel. The birthday was the same as Logan's and things started to feel strange to him. The name of the infant child was stated as "Logan Freel." A sense of dread welled up in his gut and he wanted to run and pretend he had never come here and lie to the caller and tell him there was nothing to find. There was no way what he was seeing was the truth.

The last thing he saw in the box, only as he glanced away from the medical report in disgust, was a newspaper clipping that he didn't really care about until he saw the picture that was folded under the crease. Unfurling the page, he stared in horror at the three men standing with the height chart to their backs and the sinister smiles on their faces. They had been arrested, and he never knew that. It was never spoken about after he went to live with Able. He reached behind him and grabbed the other image. It was the same men, though in the picture with Able they were a bit younger, as was he. According to the article they had been arrested, tried, and sentenced to life in prison for the home invasion murders of Martin and Judith Aster.

Suddenly, it all made more than perfect sense to Logan. Martin and Judith were not his parents. They never were. His real dad had always been Able. His mother was a woman he had never met and probably never would. He pieced together the worst part and it crushed him. The men in the pictures were the same ones and they were with Able because Able had something to do with the deaths of his parents…or what he thought his whole life were his parents anyway. He didn't know how he was involved, but it made sense. He didn't know how he had come to live with the Asters or to adopt their name. His first name had always been the same, and that was odd too. The more he thought about things, the more confusing they became. His whole existence had become a lie in a matter of hours.

He finished with the boxes and found nothing near as damning as the evidence that he was not who he thought he was because the man that raised him had been a deception. He wanted to go back in time knowing what he did and start over with Able. Treat him like a father from the start and not fight with him like he hated him. Some part of him was glad the old man was dead, though, because he had a desire, slight as it was, to kill the man for all of his lies and dishonesty as well. He packed everything in the biggest box he could find, forcing some of it to fit since there was so much. The medical report and newspaper article were the first items he would come across when it was opened. He tossed it in the car and headed for home.

Once a week had passed, Logan received the call he was promised. He answered it a lot less exuberantly than he had the first time. He didn't speak this time, leaving the conversation opening to the man on the other end. He didn't have to wait long.

"Did you find what I sent you to look for?" he asked.

Logan thought about lying and saying it had all been a wild goose chase, but he thought better of that idea. It was obvious from his hesitance to speak and his quiet voice that something wasn't the same between the times of the two calls. Anyone with any sense would have noticed it. "I found it…or I found something."

"I bet you did. How did it feel to learn your whole life was a big lie?"

"It felt like someone ripped out my soul. How the fuck do you think it felt?"

"I know exactly how it felt. It was the same feeling I had when I found out that my family had lied to me my whole life."

"You went through the same thing? I don't understand."

"Put simply, you aren't the only one. A little more detail informs you that Able Lock, or Harold Franklyn, or fucking Bruce Goddard in my case, was a father to many kids. You were the only one he was capable of getting back to raise the way he wanted. The rest of us were hiding, we just didn't know it."

"I still don't fully get what you are saying to me. Forgive me, but it just isn't registering."

"Mr. Aster, what I am saying is that Able Lock was a madman. He fathered many kids to build an army of sorts. The mothers ran from him, taking the kids and disappearing into the void. He found yours, and when they were killed, he simply took you back home with him."

"Why did no one ask any questions then? If I was taken from my family, why did no one come looking for me?"

"You still aren't there, but you are getting closer. No one asked questions because you were taken from a family who never had kids of their own. They didn't have children that anyone knew of and when you went missing, no one noticed because as far as they knew, you were never there."

"Oh, my god. He didn't kidnap me. He took me back. He didn't raise me as his own after my father died. He raised me like that because I was his."

"Now, you're there. So, I want you to help me figure out who he was, and what all the secrecy was about."

"That's not something I care to know, honestly," said Logan.

"A man like that is going to have enemies. His are going to become ours."

"They haven't been in thirty years. Why would they be now?"

"Because I just told them everything they needed to know."

"What?" The word had barely exited his mouth when there was a muffled gunshot from the other end of the line. Then there were a couple more. The air was dead for a few seconds and then a new voice came on the line.

"Mr. Aster…or Freel since we are using real names now. We found him. You cannot hide forever. Your father was a bad man. If only you knew."

"I know nothing about my father, apparently."

"You know enough to understand that he wasn't who he said he was."

"I trusted him when I shouldn't have. I see that now."

"It's so much more than that. You were always a part of his bigger plan, and now it is in progress. I guess there is only one thing left to say, Mr. Freel, or Aster if you prefer."

"I prefer Aster. I was raised that way."

"Fine, Mr. Aster. I have one more thing to say. See you soon."

THE END